A RHYTHMS OF REDEMPTION NOVELLA

An Awestruck Christmas Medley

EMILY CONRAD

Library of Congress Control Number: 2021914117

This is a work of fiction. Names, characters, places, and incidents are either the products of the author's imagination or are used fictitiously. Any resemblance to actual persons, living or dead, businesses, or actual events is purely coincidental. Any real locations named are used fictitiously.

Scripture quotations are from The ESV® Bible (The Holy Bible, English Standard Version®), copyright © 2001 by Crossway, a publishing ministry of Good News Publishers. Used by permission. All rights reserved.

ISBN 978-1-7360388-2-6 (Paperback Edition)

ISBN 978-1-7360388-3-3 (Ebook Edition)

Cover and title page design by Okay Creations, LLC

Edited by Robin Patchen, Robin's Red Pen

Author photograph by Kim Hoffman

Visit the author's website at EmilyConradAuthor.com.

For all the Awestruck fans. I hope you enjoy tagging along for Christmas as much as I did.

1

*S*hoppers packed the escalator as tightly as a rush-hour subway car.

Gannon must not have been the only one struggling to find the perfect gift.

Chicago's Michigan Avenue, with some of the best shopping in the world, was failing him. He'd been in and out of at least a dozen stores, yet he'd seen nothing that would come close to correcting what had gone off course between him and Adeline. Even this four-story mall hadn't slowed him down long enough for his winter hat and coat to get uncomfortable. Few of the boutiques garnered even a second glance.

The escalator carried him from one garland-decked corridor to a nearly identical one a level down. He followed John, his band's drummer—and his closest friend—off at the bottom.

Nicole, John's girlfriend, pointed a mittened hand toward the sparkling display at an upscale jewelry store. "Women love diamonds."

When he and John had described Adeline's tastes, they'd used the words "down to earth." Either Nicole was out of touch with what that meant, or she intended her suggestions to steer John, not help Gannon.

The drummer cut Gannon a loaded glance that said he'd guessed the same. But a smile crept across John's face, so apparently, he didn't mind.

"Oh, come on." Nicole stood in the store's doorway, her back to the guard stationed at the entrance. "Every woman loves jewelry. Even the ones who like the simple things." Her mittens obscured the movement, but judging by the way she lifted her hands, he guessed she'd put air quotes around *simple things*.

The guard eyed them as they followed Nicole in, probably because Gannon and John didn't fit the profile of their usual clientele. Gannon wore an old sweatshirt under his coat, and he had the hood up over the top of his knit cap. A pair of non-prescription glasses completed the disguise, which so far had kept him from being recognized. John wore a nice enough black jacket, but tears decorated his jeans, and the soles of his shoes were separating from the leather.

Only Nicole looked like she belonged. The model had drawn stares all evening, and Gannon wished they could've talked her into washing off her makeup, pulling her hair into a bun, and trading her designer labels for something boxy and ill-fitting. Even then, she'd probably garner attention.

She whipped off her mittens as she approached the nearest counter. Overhead, ornaments dangled from the ceiling, slowly turning with the air from the heating vents. Nicole's hair shimmered as she looked back, one finger on the glass surface. "See? Easy. She'd love it."

Before Gannon could focus long enough to identify which necklace she meant to indicate, Nicole found something else.

Gannon looked to John for help.

The drummer excelled at figuring people out, a skill that enabled him to pick fitting gifts, as evidenced by half of the many shopping bags he carried. The other half belonged to Nicole.

Still smiling, John stepped around him. He passed his shopping bags to one hand, put an arm around Nicole's waist, and murmured in her ear. She flashed Gannon a smile as John ushered her away, and they browsed the other side of the store.

Space wasn't the help Gannon wanted. He needed the perfect gift for Adeline. Being on tour as their relationship turned serious had been less than ideal. He loved her and hated being apart, but they'd been battling conflicting schedules, long flights, bad internet, and jet lag all year.

She'd first complained of the distance back in May. He'd fit in a few extra visits and coaxed her into catching up with him at a couple of tour stops, but by Thanksgiving, the strain mounted, waiting for the first excuse to unleash havoc.

An excuse he'd supplied—accidentally, of course—but supplied, nonetheless.

He wandered the shop, studying the selection. Though tempting, jewelry felt even more generic than the other gifts he already had waiting at the cabin. He needed something uniquely suited to Adeline, the woman who saw his faults and loved him anyway.

A cross necklace glittered under the lights. Adeline challenged his faith by the way she lived out her own, but a small, sparkly, outward symbol didn't do justice to the bedrock they were building their lives on.

He advanced down the counter.

Engagement rings?

His steps halted. He'd love to put a ring on her finger and jump into a future together.

To have and to hold ... The snatch of a wedding ceremony sounded like the opposite of what they'd experienced this year.

His phone buzzed, and his mouth turned dry at the sight of

Adeline's name on the display. What would she say if she could see him considering rings?

He hit the button to answer while peering through the glass. She'd probably appreciate the simple style of the tear-shaped diamond on the plain band, and a rock that size might eliminate her worries about his priorities. "Hey."

"Hi." Her flat tone made a disappointing contrast to the sparkly jewelry in front of him. "Is John with you? He's not answering his phone, and I can't find the list of which dog gets which supplement with dinner."

"Yeah, sure."

Because they planned to all spend Christmas Eve together, John's dogs, who'd boarded with a trainer most of the tour, waited for their master with Adeline this evening.

Awestruck's visit to Wisconsin would be short. On December twenty-sixth, the band would pile back on a plane and power through the last two weeks of the year-long tour. Two days wouldn't provide much opportunity to rebuild burned bridges.

Since John and his girlfriend spoke with an associate right now, Gannon lingered by the rings, hoping to do a little bridge repair. The cluster of three diamonds was a nice symbol. *A cord of three strands is not easily broken.* "We're in Chicago, and I'm in this jewelry store—"

Barking on Adeline's end of the line interrupted.

"What?" Frustration lined her voice.

Her inability to hear may've been a gift, because suddenly, he couldn't imagine her saying yes and offering her finger for a ring if he brought one of these to her.

"Is Camo the one that gets the digestive enzymes or Trigger?" Another bark added an exclamation point to her question.

Gannon turned from the rings. "Hang on."

He collected the answer from John as Nicole followed the associate toward the register.

"Trigger," Gannon said into the phone.

"Great. Thanks." Her clipped words didn't convey everything he knew to be true of her. She was creative, thoughtful, and hard-working. Not caught up in the trappings of fame and fortune.

He'd inadvertently exposed her to the pitfalls of both.

"Hey, look—"

Simultaneously, Adeline said, "I've got to go."

The yaps of hungry dogs underscored the point.

With a sigh, Gannon said goodbye and disconnected.

He considered retracing his steps to the engagement rings, but a wedding wouldn't solve the distance between them. Her work would keep her in Lakeshore while his sent him around the world. If they married, she wouldn't need to support herself, of course, but Adeline wanted to make a difference in the world, and her job played an important role in that. He couldn't ask her to quit to shadow him all the time.

So, no engagement ring for them this Christmas.

Gannon met John and Nicole at the register as Nicole passed her credit card to the associate.

"No luck?" John asked.

Gannon studied the bustling corridor. "The first diamond she's going to get from me will be an engagement ring, and after what happened at Thanksgiving, this isn't the time."

"We have a little more time."

Gannon would've preferred John to argue about the timing instead of confirming.

The associate slid the card back to Nicole. "I'm sorry, ma'am, but this card declined."

"Try this one." Nicole pulled out another and flashed a smile. "I'm from LA. You'd think my bank would be used to me traveling by now."

They ought to be. Nicole traveled as much as Awestruck, though her career took her different places.

The night they'd met her, she'd dropped into conversation that she lived debt-free. The mention seemed both casual and true to Gannon at the time. But now?

"I'm so sorry." The associate shook her head as she returned the second card.

John's expression darkened.

To give them privacy, Gannon excused himself and scoped out nearby stores. When the couple rejoined him, Nicole carried a robin's-egg blue bag from the jewelry store, her trademark smile in place. Annoyance marked John's expression.

Trouble in paradise?

Gannon ran his thumbs along the inside edge of his knit cap, then pushed through the shopping center's door and into the freezing air of downtown Chicago.

They wove around other shoppers until Gannon slowed in front of yet another gilded window display. He should've brought Adeline here to shop for herself. Michigan Avenue could pass for romantic with all the Christmas decorations. Maybe even romantic enough that she wouldn't mind picking out her own gift.

John cleared his throat. "At least she didn't give you a price limit."

Gannon blinked and realized which store he'd stopped before.

Right.

A three-thousand-dollar purse wouldn't get him out of this hole.

"What would show her that I care and that I'm committed?" The two accusations she'd lobbed at him the last time he'd seen her.

She'd apologized shortly after, but he understood where

the comments came from. He hated the distance his job forced between them as much as she did.

John smirked, and they continued down the street. "Not falling asleep during Thanksgiving dinner would've been a start."

"This is serious."

John clapped his shoulder. "You two are going to be fine. The tour's almost over. That's the real issue."

If so, they had a couple of more weeks to endure, and Gannon couldn't bear waiting that long to set things right between them.

Besides, there would be other tours.

He and Adeline needed more than a great Christmas. They needed a plan to stay better connected in the future, one that would lead to a very different trip to the jewelry counter.

This gift would be the first step toward that one—if he chose well.

His line of sight caught on a stuffed dog in the window of the next store. Adeline loved animals so much that she'd fostered dogs and cats for her local shelter before adopting Bruce, the sweet old lab who followed her constantly. "A puppy?"

John made a face and shook his head before a text stole his attention.

"Tim?" Gannon asked.

"Mm-hm." The drummer typed a reply to their band's manager and slid the device back into his pocket.

"What time is it?"

"Seven thirty."

Gannon winced. One hour to find a gift—the perfect gift—and get to the pre-show meet and greet. He shouldn't have put off shopping until the last minute, but every time he'd considered it—almost daily since Thanksgiving—he'd told himself he'd think of something. Something special. Something meaningful.

The delay had only played up the importance of this gift, making the decision even more impossible than at the start.

"Put a bow on the house," John said.

"Funny." On one of Gannon's trips to Wisconsin a couple of months before, she'd helped him pick the house he'd move into after the tour ended, when the band would officially make Lakeshore their home. Because he did plan to marry her, they'd shared the decision, but that didn't mean he could call the place a gift. "I hope she likes one of the basses."

"She will, but she'll insist you return two."

He'd bought three upright double basses because each instrument possessed a unique sound. If only he knew her well enough to determine which she'd prefer. That's what the second gift—or fourth, if one counted each bass separately—would be about. He wanted to show he cared enough to have noticed her preferences.

He wanted to prove that down the line, when he brought her a ring, a future with him would make her happy.

All those basses proved was his ability to spend money.

"Kate's getting married." As John mentioned the fact about his sister, he tipped his head toward a three-story kitchen and home furnishing store across the street. "I want to get her a knife set."

"To arm her in case it doesn't work out?"

Nicole laughed.

"Her knives cut like forks." John took the lead through the slush and across the street. "She said when she gets a house, she wants to host some holidays."

Gannon puzzled the pieces together. "And she's moving in with Tanner when she gets married, so she'll have the house, but not the knives, and you don't want to have to saw through turkey with a knife that cuts like a fork."

"I knew you'd catch up." Bells tied to the door jingled as John pulled the handle.

Gannon considered continuing down the street alone, hunting for a store that seemed more Adeline's style, but they'd already passed dozens of stores, and not one stocked the perfect gift. Someone might as well be happy, and since John seemed to be the only one with any idea which gifts would please their recipients, Gannon followed his lead.

~

JOHN WANTED companionship and a family of his own, but here he was, with a woman he wasn't sure he could trust.

She'd claimed all along to live within her means. Over Thanksgiving, he'd learned of her student loans. "But those don't count," she'd said. "They were for education."

He'd let it go. With her income, she could pay off student loans anytime she wanted, and it wasn't his place to judge her for making payments instead of clearing the books.

How would she excuse maxed-out credit cards?

Not that he'd asked if that had caused the problem back in the jewelry store.

Instead, he'd bought the bracelet for her. He didn't want to fight at Christmas, when they were on the verge of having a couple of days off together. After spending the twenty-fourth at the cabin with the others, he and Nicole would drive down to spend Christmas day with his sisters and parents. The visit would make her the first girl he'd brought home since setting off with the band at age eighteen.

"You know anything about knives?" He glanced at Nicole.

She was beautiful, but John wouldn't date her if she weren't also intelligent, upbeat, and kind.

Early in the tour, Awestruck did some interviews with a non-profit endeavoring to end childhood bullying. Nicole's own spots for the same campaign had been filmed the same day, and she and John hit it off. That night, she'd surprised him by attending Awestruck's show.

Now, she hoisted a hopeful smile. "You get what you pay for?"

John grimaced. "I'm going to need more to go on."

Laughing, she led a charge toward the appropriate area of the store and wrangled a salesperson to help with recommendations.

As the clerk rattled off options, John tried to get eyes on Gannon. No luck.

Gannon probably still intended to find the perfect gift—and maybe he would, since he always seemed to pull things off at the last minute—but more likely, one of two other things would happen. Either the crowd would recognize Gannon and they'd never get out of this mess of last-minute shoppers, or the lead singer would check the weather.

The brewing storm, and not the meet and greet, had been the subject of Tim's text. Thankfully, at least so far, Gannon's search for the perfect gift had kept him from realizing he might not make it up north to give Adeline a gift of any kind, perfect or otherwise.

Tim wanted to keep the blizzard from Gannon until after the show, and John didn't see the point in rocking the boat. They wouldn't learn until later if the plane they'd chartered could make the flight. Why worry prematurely when they couldn't control the situation?

The clerk thumped her hand on a box. "What do you think?"

John had missed everything she'd said. He looked to Nicole for help.

The bracelet glittered on her wrist as she pointed to one of the options. "I'd go with top-rated and lifetime guarantee."

"Sold."

He carried the box to the line at the register, about fifteen people deep. While waiting, he sent a message to their driver to pick them up in front of the store in a few minutes. He slid his phone in his pocket and spotted Gannon at a different register, no one in line behind him. He must've played the rock star card to get someone to open a lane.

A man complained as John bypassed the line, but John pretended not to hear. The sooner they got out of there, the better. Interacting with a crowd on Michigan Avenue would make them late for the fans who'd shelled out for backstage passes.

"What did you find?" Nicole bounced to Gannon's side and peered into the black-and-white bag the clerk set on the counter. She moved aside some tissue paper, glanced in, and stepped back, looking puzzled.

Gannon flashed a conspiratorial smile to the sales lady, who beamed back at him.

The clerk shifted her focus. "And what do you have?" Her expression went a little too neutral at the sight of the knife set.

A random cashier might not be impressed, but John knew his family—knew Kate—and this was a good gift. One he'd wrap and deliver himself, unlike the gifts he'd given so many other years, which he'd ordered online and shipped.

As they stepped back onto the dark street, flurries floated down and melted underfoot. John glanced to see if Gannon might've started to consider the weather, only to find his friend's gaze on him.

"What?"

Gannon glanced at Nicole without speaking, but those raised eyebrows filled in the question. He wanted to know what happened in the jewelry store.

John too. But her cards may have declined for the reason she'd said—travel. He was bringing her to meet his family. He didn't want to be the guy who'd assume the worst. "I'm sure it's fine."

The eyebrows quirked higher.

A black car pulled up to the curb, and Gannon got the door before the driver had the chance. John dumped the bags in the trunk, piled in the back seat with Nicole, and took her hand.

Her eyes reminded him of a lion's, shaped so her glares became downright fierce and her approval glittering. For reaching out to her, he earned a smile.

He'd so easily assured Gannon he and Adeline would be fine, and now he needed to believe the same about his own relationship. Romances ran into snags sometimes, but they didn't have to spell disaster. Negative assumptions would do them no favors.

Instead, trust and hope would carry them through.

She ran a finger along his jaw, and he kissed her cheek.

If ever there was a time for hope, Christmas had to be it.

2

*H*e shouldn't be nervous to see his own kids.

Philip cracked his knuckles and stretched his arms. Tim, Awestruck's manager, stood in a corner, phone to his ear. Across the green room, Kyle, whom Awestruck hired to play second guitar at shows, perused the snack table. Though the venue stocked the waiting area with everything Awestruck's backstage rider listed, Philip didn't have the stomach to join him.

Dad, Joan, and the kids should be here any moment. The app on Philip's phone said their flight safely landed almost an hour ago, despite the impending blizzard that had kept Tim on the phone all evening.

Philip scrubbed his hands over his face. He'd trimmed his beard short, following his jawline in the style Clare used to prefer. The style he'd preferred too until Clare's death.

Now, whenever he looked like this, every glance in a mirror reminded him of the way she used to brush his cheek with the backs of her fingers, compliment him, and wait an inch away until he couldn't resist kissing her.

Facing the grief of those memories was better than looking

in his children's eyes and seeing their fear, as he had over Thanksgiving.

He hadn't anticipated the consequences when he'd joined some of the crew in No Shave November. Letting his hair grow long too compounded the mistake. When he showed up at Dad and Joan's house for the holiday, his stepmom answered the door with the kids in tow. He'd opened his arms to hug them, but seven-year-old Nila clutched Joan's hand. Nason, younger by about two years, ran off without recognizing him.

His own kids.

He'd shaved immediately, gotten a haircut on Black Friday.

"This blizzard is a mess." Tim appeared at his side. "Why are you all so intent on living up in the sticks?"

John and Gannon wanted to move to Wisconsin. Out of gratitude for his place in the band, Philip had followed Gannon's lead and bought a place near Lakeshore, Wisconsin. Besides, the area would be a quiet and safe place to raise Nason and Nila, and he wanted them to have a peaceful childhood, like Philip's own in Iowa.

Except, Philip had been raised by two parents, while his kids would be stuck with only him after the tour ended.

The door opened, and his heart jumped, but it wasn't Nason and Nila. Just the return of the shopping party. Gannon grabbed a water bottle, and John and Nicole joined Philip. They'd barely acknowledged each other before security ushered a group of fans into the room, fidgeting, grinning, and bouncing.

What had happened to the standard warning? Usually, security gave the band time to retreat behind the autograph tables. All the extra people would intimidate the kids too, as if Philip needed more working against the reunion. Hopefully, they wouldn't arrive until after the room cleared again.

Gannon, closest to the door and the most public member of the band, got swamped first. Then, a woman separated from the group and headed for Philip and John. A trickle of others followed.

"Have fun, boys." Nicole pecked John's cheek and retreated to a chair, a smile on her face, clearly proud her boyfriend garnered so much attention.

Philip ducked the hands of the first woman, who seemed to interpret his fresh haircut as an invitation for fingers. Her touch landed on his shoulder, while another fan sidled up beside him and snapped a selfie almost before he knew what was happening.

Would Clare be proud of him like Nicole was of John? Or jealous? Angry at the liberties fans took? He'd worked with some well-known bands while she'd been alive, but in roles like Kyle's, where he played when needed without becoming an official band member or part of the creative process. Signing on with Awestruck during the creation of their biggest album yet and embarking on a world tour with them was the realization of all his dreams—career-wise, anyway.

Tim and security extricated the band—who slid quickly behind their table—and facilitated a Q and A before they allowed the fans to advance again for autographs and selfies. Bouncers quietly but carefully presided over the entire affair.

A lanky guy with deep circles under his bloodshot eyes whipped his shirt off and laid the garment on the table for the band to sign. The tracks on his arms filled in a far-too-common story. After John signed, Philip straightened the material to add his name. Before the felt tip of the marker darkened the fabric, a gentle hand touched his biceps.

"Daddy?" Seven-year-old Nila peered at him with round eyes. Her sweet mouth split into a grin that showed off the progress of her first two adult teeth, a new blank space on one side of them.

Philip pulled her onto his lap. A barrette shaped like holly held back her curly brown hair on one side. A big metallic heart adorned the center of her sweater, and a small, heart-shaped locket dangled from her neck.

Beyond her, the addict loomed.

What had he been thinking, inviting the kids to a place like this?

Philip scribbled his name on the fabric and pushed the shirt back.

Awestruck might be clean, but the world of rock and roll wasn't. Drugs and sex were never far off. Walk into the wrong room backstage, and who knew what they'd witness.

By the door, Nason cowered by Dad's side, and Joan shifted, hugely out of place in a sweatshirt printed with a cardinal-dotted winter scene.

The meet and greet was almost over, and then everyone but Awestruck would head out as the support band took the stage and started the show. For now, he had a job to do.

Still holding Nila, he scooted closer to the table.

John flipped one of the band photographs they were signing and handed Nila a marker. "I miss my dogs, but I don't get to see them until tomorrow. Could you draw me one?"

"Sure." She pulled the cap off a permanent marker. Not ideal, but the entertainment would keep her from paying too much attention to the fans.

John didn't even have kids, and he possessed better parenting instincts than Philip.

Philip looked to his dad, now by the snack table. His strategy appeared to be distracting Nason with sugar. A crew member decked out in a Santa hat approached them and produced a toy truck from who-knew-where.

Philip should've brought toys, should've realized being in the same room with him wouldn't be enough to keep the kids happy, should've known they'd need entertainment. Clare would've known.

Now, Philip needed to be both mother and father to his

kids, but he wasn't fooling anyone—least of all himself. He wasn't cut out for this.

∽

SHE NEVER SHOULD'VE ASSURED Tegan this would be easy. Adeline set down the craft scissors, arched her back, and splayed her fingers.

Three pairs of brown eyes watched her with concern. If only the dogs could pitch in with making these wedding favors.

She'd cut thirty-six decorative squares from the scrapbook paper, which meant she had sixty-four to go. Afterward, she'd have to punch two holes in each of the one hundred squares.

The whole time she'd been cutting, she'd been reading the printed text over and over.

Love Burns Bright
Drew and Tegan
Despite her joy for her friends, the suggestion that love ought to burn brightly stung.

As if sensing her disquietude, John's brindle pit bull pushed onto his stocky legs and lumbered over to nuzzle her hand. As she petted Camo's head, she eyed the other two dogs. Her old lab, Bruce, snored with his eyes open. John's other dog, a gray pit named Trigger, turned a circle and lay back down.

Tegan padded into the rustic dining room of the cabin Gannon rented for Christmas. Adeline's roommate and best friend wore jeans and a cute sweater rather than the pajamas she'd wear at home because the guys would arrive in a few hours.

Adeline could only imagine the inconveniences Tegan's decision to keep her company tonight caused, considering the wedding was only a week away. Yet Tegan refused to allow Adeline to drive an hour through the snowstorm alone.

Neither of them voiced the fact that, if she arrived at the

cabin solo, she might've spent more than the drive on her own. The snow might prevent Awestruck from leaving Chicago tonight. If they had to cut the two-day visit down to one, would the trip be worthwhile?

Tegan rounded the table, and her fuzzy reindeer socks came into view. "You are a saint."

Camo blinked at Tegan, seemed to conclude his job was done, and went back to bed.

Adeline hadn't intended to be this saintly, but as the maid of honor, she refused to complain just because she'd once again underestimated the difficulty of a DIY project. "They're going to be really cute. It'll be a beautiful send-off."

Tegan took the chair next to hers. "What can I do?"

"You don't have to do anything. I still have a week."

"That week includes Christmas and a visit from your boyfriend. When Drew and I decided on a New Year's Eve wedding, I didn't consider how close that would put it to Christmas."

"You didn't have many days to choose from." The day Drew landed the pastoral position in Colorado, he'd proposed to Tegan and asked her to move with him. Eight weeks later, here they were. As soon as they returned from their honeymoon in January, they'd relocate.

"Still." Tegan claimed one of the scalloped-edged squares Adeline cut and lined up the hole punch with the first little circle. The tool clicked through the paper, and Tegan turned it to make the second hole. She threaded the square onto a sparkler and dropped the stick into the vase. "One down. Ninety-nine to go." She snickered. "Reminds me of a certain song."

When the newlyweds left the reception, everyone would light their sparklers and line up outside to see them off. The photographs would be gorgeous, but planning to stand out in the cold to bid the couple farewell might've been as ill-conceived as this craft project.

Tegan punched another hole. "Are you worried?"

"About what?"

"The snow. Gannon, and whether he'll make it."

"Not much we can do about it." Even if he canceled, Adeline and Tegan would be safer weathering the storm at the cabin than to attempt returning to Lakeshore tonight.

The cabin was nicer than their house anyway. Lots of flannel blankets and wood furnishings. Christmas decorations graced every possible surface. A giant fireplace faced cozy couches and chairs. The biggest wreath she'd ever seen hung out front. The kitchen brimmed with comfort foods and six varieties of hot cocoa. Enough bedrooms waited down the hall for her and Tegan, each member of Awestruck, and Philip's parents and kids.

But Adeline didn't want impressive.

She wanted time with Gannon.

"You can say you're frustrated."

Frustrated didn't seem like the right word.

"Being apart is harder than I expected." She carried a constant ache to be with him. If he missed a call, showed up jet-lagged, or canceled altogether, that ache easily morphed into suspicion that he didn't miss or prioritize her the way she did him.

She wasn't proud of the way she'd reacted when he'd nodded off at Thanksgiving dinner.

She'd much rather spend the precious moments with him in his arms, not arguing. He wanted the same, or he wouldn't have apologized so quickly for completely justifiable fatigue. He'd traveled a third of the globe to show up.

The visit ended with a kiss that felt more obligatory than sincere, and the memory of it did little to warm her now.

If love burned brightly, like these wedding favors claimed, it ought to pierce the darkness caused by distance.

It didn't.

She turned the paper in her hand, cutting along the line.

"All this wedding stuff can't be easy for you."

"I'm happy for you. Drew's a lucky guy, and you're going to be happy together."

"Together being the operative word."

Adeline blinked hard, focusing on the wrought-iron chandelier over the table. Evergreen boughs graced the decorative metal scrolls. Between those and the real tree in the living room, the whole place smelled of pine.

"He loves you." Tegan spoke gently, so why was Adeline struggling to keep it together? Tegan touched her hand. "And you love him, or time apart wouldn't hurt this way."

Love wasn't supposed to hurt or leave her lonely.

Losing her roommate weeks before Gannon moved to Lakeshore didn't help. Neither did the knowledge that, if all went well, touring would be part of Gannon's life for years to come.

She ran her wrist under her eye. "Sorry. Pity party. I'm going to miss you."

Tegan offered a regretful smile. "I'll miss you too. But God has good things in store for both of us. You and Gannon simply need a better way to handle travel. Why don't you go with him more?"

"I work."

"So quit. I know I talked you into that job at the college, and I stand by that. It was a good decision at the time, but things change."

"What kind of meaning would my life have stuffed away in a hotel, following him around?"

Tegan shrugged. "For this to be realistic long term, you

need to either come to terms with the distance or eliminate it. My vote's for eliminating."

Adeline agreed—in theory—but they may not succeed at eliminating the distance for Christmas, let alone into the future.

~

YEARS AGO, John earned a few bruises by struggling against Gannon and Matt, Awestruck's first bassist, when they'd gleefully helped a stylist fasten bracelets on John's arms for a photoshoot. Now, he'd worn the leather cuff and braided cords on stages around the world. They'd become part of the persona that separated his true identity from his role as Awestruck's drummer.

On stage, John acted as if he didn't mind cameras in his face. He acted as if he thrived on noise. As if he cared enough about fashion to tie and buckle an assortment of leather around his arms every day—and one or two cords around his neck for good measure.

Offstage, he was—and wanted to remain—someone fans wouldn't even recognize. Reserved. Loyal. Content. The absence of accessories had become part of that.

So, after realizing he'd forgotten the bracelets, he spent the rest of the meet and greet rubbing his exposed wrists. As soon as the opening band took the stage, he headed straight for his dressing room.

Crossing the space, he checked his phone and found a text from his real estate agent.

This new listing might be worth considering, for the land if nothing else. She'd included a link.

Because the band was moving to northern Wisconsin, he had to find a house. He'd already passed on so many properties, he would end up staying in California or at Gannon's for a while after the tour. Maybe he should've built to begin with, but the undertaking had sounded like more of a hassle.

Standing by the vanity, he tapped through the slideshow of the property. The older home appeared well-maintained. Quiet. Homey. He texted back to set up an appointment while he'd be in the area on Christmas Eve.

As he tightened the first of the bracelets on his wrist, he realized he'd have to bring Nicole along to the showing. She wouldn't be impressed by the pictures, but if she first saw the house in person, she might give it a fair chance.

"Excuse me. John?" A woman dressed in a blazer and slacks stood in the doorway behind him. Her stilettos clicked as she stepped into the room.

He grabbed the leather cuff off the vanity and worked on the buckle. "Can I help you?"

One of the woman's carefully groomed eyebrows arched. "I wondered if you might share Nicole."

Nicole? "If you're a reporter—"

The woman waved her fingers, dismissing his suspicion. With an extended hand, she stepped toward him. "Renee Belvedere. I work for the agency that represents Nicole."

Her skin was cool, her shake firm. John already liked her no better than the man who usually facilitated Nicole's business dealings.

"What can I do for you?" He held his wrist against his ribs to keep one final braided cord in place while he secured the ends.

"Help us talk Nicole into working? You seem to be the only person she shows up for."

He shook his head, confused. If she wanted to book Nicole for a gig over Christmas, she'd chosen her ally poorly. Between charity events, stages, and photoshoots, he and Nicole had shared little time away from the spotlight. A private, low-key

Christmas would serve as a good foundation toward a more authentic relationship.

"Your darling has missed several jobs."

As if he could speak for her.

"She has obligations in January, but if she keeps skipping out, we won't be able to do much for her or her career. When a company books Nicole Deering, they expect Nicole Deering. Getting someone else last minute tends to leave a sour taste."

He finished the last knot and lowered his hands, twisting his wrists to settle everything into place. The new information about Nicole fit a little too well with the declined cards.

Exactly how much was Nicole hiding from him? And why?

Regardless of the answers, he wouldn't hazard getting in the middle of a dispute between her and her agency. "She's here. Talk to her."

"I will, but it might be helpful if you had a word with her before she throws her career away."

The gravity in the woman's voice seeped like poison into his hopes for a nice Christmas.

No. There was a logical explanation for it all. Nicole would talk to him about this—and the declined cards—when she was ready, and when she did, it would all make sense.

3

*W*hen the show ended, Philip exited the stage and handed his bass to his tech. His father waited for him in the wings. Somewhere along the line tonight, Dad had picked up a necklace of working Christmas lights, which caused a laugh to bubble up from Philip's chest. "Where are the kids?"

Belatedly, his father dipped his head closer to hear over the racket of the crowd. When Philip was about to repeat himself, Dad replied. "Sleeping. It's pretty late for them." Dad clapped him on the shoulder. "Great show. The pyrotechnics were out of this world."

"You should see the guy who makes them happen." Rumor had it that Sparky—whose arguments he should be called Fireball fell on deaf ears—kept his head shaved because he'd singed his hair too many times. "I'd introduce you, but he's probably rushing to get to Christmas with his family."

"Tim says no one's taking off from Chicago."

Philip cringed. "Did he come up with a different plan to head north?"

"Like what?"

Philip shrugged. Gannon didn't accept no as an answer easily. If there was a way to get to the cabin as planned, he'd find it. "I'll clean up, and we'll see what's going on."

He pushed into the dressing room. As his eyes landed on the trio on the couch, he stopped. Joan sat in the middle, wearing a necklace that matched Dad's. The lights blinked away as she snored, head tilted back, as asleep as the kids on either side of her. Nason and Nila each lay with one of Philip's jackets covering their small frames. Philip had thought Nason outgrew sucking his thumb, but apparently not. The fan of Nila's eyelashes on her cheeks reminded him of Clare.

How much would she resemble her mother when she got older? And how would Philip cope with that?

"They lasted about halfway through the show," Dad whispered.

Philip had wanted to share what he did with the kids, but so much for his hopes that they'd enjoy the experience. He checked his watch. Closing in on eleven.

He'd grab that shower and see if Tim booked them rooms locally or found a way to the cabin as planned.

"She hasn't been sleeping well."

He followed his dad's line of sight to Nila.

His princess. The strongest reminder of Clare he had.

"Why?"

"Upset about moving. She's been having nightmares about being all alone."

"I'll be there." But even he understood that would be little comfort in the face of leaving the security of Joan and Dad's house.

"The change is hard. She's been at that school for a year, has friends, and knows what to expect." Dad's tone held no judgment.

That didn't stop the information from cutting deep. "And Nason?"

"Kindergarten is new to him, and he hasn't caught on that moving in the middle of a year isn't normal."

Philip had moved his kids around a lot. Until Clare's death four years ago, they'd lived in LA. After, nothing clicked.

He and the kids moved to Iowa to be close to his parents in the hope that Dad and Joan would act as training wheels, so one day, Philip could parent alone. But Iowa meant few career opportunities. Nothing helpful or healthy stepped forward to fill the yawning emptiness.

He needed to work, and not solely for the money.

After a year, he moved the children back to LA, still little better at relating to them. Working again felt good and necessary, and he'd managed to limit his travel, rarely leaving for more than one week out of each month. Even then, their beloved nanny cared for them while he traveled.

Then came Awestruck.

As he'd seen yet again tonight, being on tour wasn't the best place for a kid. So, he'd sent them to live with their grandparents.

No nanny. No tutor. Just regular school and Dad and Joan.

Naturally, Nila preferred to stay in that situation, but he missed her and Nason. Especially on seeing them like this, his body ached for the trusting, comforting weight of their sleeping forms snuggled to his chest, heads leaned on his shoulders. And when they were awake, wrestling matches with Nason and Nila's sweet kisses on his cheeks served as the antidote to too many lonely nights in generic hotel rooms.

The kids gave him company, comfort, purpose.

But what did he give them?

Nightmares?

He loved them. He'd do anything for them.

Even ...

His heartbeat seemed to stop, his lungs froze as a new idea dropped into place.

Even ask Dad and Joan to take them, not for a year, but permanently?

The idea reeked of loneliness, shame, and failure.

But he wasn't a good father. What if the most loving, selfless act he could do as a father was to let someone else raise them?

You don't have to decide right now.

The words came to him in Clare's voice, an echo of what she'd said while they were dating, when she'd revealed her desire to have kids someday. He'd hoped to marry her, but kids?

The idea grew on him. He'd wanted Clare to have everything she dreamed of.

His kids deserved the same, whatever the cost to him.

He drew a measured breath and ran his hand through his freshly cut hair. Even he could smell that he needed the shower. "Give me ten minutes."

~

GANNON WANTED to deliver the gift he'd found, and more importantly, he'd made a promise to Adeline. He wouldn't fail to spend Christmas together over a grounded airplane. "The sooner we get on the road, the better."

Tim stayed anchored against the wall, arms crossed. "They're supposed to get eighteen inches of snow." Probably more snow than Tim, a Californian who preferred beaches, had seen in his life.

"If you think something this tall"—Gannon held his hands apart, estimating a foot and a half—"is going to stop me, you've never met me."

"You won't get tour buses through it."

"The counties up north have all the equipment they need to clear the roads. This isn't their first winter."

"Even interstates get messy in the middle of a snowstorm." This quiet warning rose from Steve, their tour manager, who sat on a couch in Gannon's dressing room. No stranger to finding ways to transport the band, often at odd hours and under a time crunch, if anyone understood the obstacle and how to overcome it, Steve did. "The country roads you'll need to take toward the end of the route might be buried pretty deep."

"What do you suggest? Flying's not an option." Gannon refocused on Tim. "Unless you want to rent snowmobiles or dog sleds, driving seems like the best option."

"Just not the buses." Steve rose from the couch, phone already in hand. "I'll make some calls. Find you guys SUVs with snow tires. Less unruly than a bus would be, and safer. Seatbelts and all."

Without waiting for responses, Steve ambled from the room.

At least someone was on board. Gannon turned back to Tim, triumphant.

"Getting there will be a huge hassle, and all for one or two days. After how badly Thanksgiving went, I'm not sure why you're all desperate for a repeat."

Because no one wanted a repeat. Every member of the band wanted to salvage relationships from the hits they'd taken in November. Philip and John didn't have to travel up north to do so, but Philip did want to show the kids the new house, and Nicole and John might benefit from a shared adventure. "You've got something better to do?"

"Nope." Tim pushed away from the wall. His ex was spending Christmas with her parents, Tim's daughter in tow, as she'd done for Thanksgiving. Probably why the guy wore all black like Halloween was two days away and not Christmas. "I just hate to see you go to all this trouble for what could be a disappointment."

"Your concern is ..."

"Unwelcome. I know."

No. The concern was sad because it stemmed from Tim's

disappointments, but he wouldn't want the pity. As the manager showed himself out, Gannon snatched his phone.

In a second, Adeline's face smiled up at him. He'd taken this picture of her back in April, when they'd finally made their relationship official. He still couldn't see that just-been-kissed smile often enough.

Beneath the image, his phone offered the options to text or call.

He hesitated.

He could break the news of the delay in a text.

The original plan had been to arrive in the middle of the night. Not showing up until morning wouldn't impact that much. But, this was one more bead in a long strand of times when he couldn't do what he'd promised on time.

He'd better call.

He dropped onto the couch and counted off three rings.

"Hi." She already sounded wary, as expectant of disappointment as Tim.

"How's the weather up there?"

A sigh. "Snowing pretty good. By you?"

"Same. Planes aren't taking off, and with how long this blizzard is supposed to last, they won't guarantee we can fly tomorrow either."

She didn't reply, and he imagined her biting her lips. If only she had enough faith in him to ask if he could find a way. Her silence suggested she expected the worst.

"We're going to drive."

"That would take seven hours in good weather."

"I'm guessing at least ten in this, which will put us there late morning. So don't wait up, but we're still coming."

"I'm not sure that's such a great idea."

She didn't want to see him?

John let himself in and plunked down on the other end of the couch.

Gannon focused on his call. On Adeline and not doing more damage. "I've been looking forward to seeing you. This is important."

"It's also dangerous." Concern warmed her tone. "The roads are awful."

Oh. So she wasn't ready to give up on the visit, on him. Relief buoyed him. "We'll be careful. They're renting SUVs that can handle the snow."

John angled toward him, interest lifting some of the fatigue from his features.

"You're sure you want to go to all this trouble?" Her voice conveyed hope.

Hope. There was hope for them, for this reunion.

"I'm sure I want to see you."

"Just make sure you get to. That there's no accident or anything."

"Will do." He pictured the cabin, all the empty rooms he'd scrolled through in the listing when he'd chosen the rental. The place better live up to the promises so Adeline would want for nothing while she waited. "You're okay for the night? Tegan's with you?"

"We're fine." For once, the often-dismissive phrase sounded sincere.

"Okay. See you tomorrow. Love you."

"I love you too." Was that a note of sadness in her voice?

He should've put his feelings for her into a full sentence, but she'd already disconnected.

He typed a message. *I love you. I will be there.*

The typed words appeared small and insignificant, but the four hundred miles between them narrowed his options. He sent the message and hoped she liked the gifts. One of the basses, at least, and the last present he'd picked up.

John sat forward. "Where are they getting SUVs?"

"I don't know. Steve's working on it." He studied his friend. "You and Nicole are doing okay?"

John shrugged. "She's meeting with someone from her agency."

"Here? Now?"

"I guess."

A knock interrupted before Gannon asked about the scene at the jewelry store. The dressing room door opened, Gannon's guitar tech stepped in, and John silently escaped.

∼

JOHN SAT at the table in the tour bus with an arm around Nicole's shoulders as he observed Steve. Their tour manager's fidgeting grin suggested he was proud of whatever travel arrangements he'd made. Proud enough to accompany them to pick up the vehicles, though he wasn't coming to the cabin.

Nic peered toward the windows, but the blinds were drawn against the snowy night. "The roads don't seem that bad."

On the surface, neither did his relationship with Nicole. But she hadn't said a word about her discussion with the woman from her agency. Then again, they'd been around others almost constantly since her meeting with Renee. When could she have shared the details?

John focused on the more immediate problem: the roads. "They'll be worse up north."

The miniature ornaments on the small tree he and Philip had duct taped to the table last week, the bus's only Christmas cheer, rocked as the wheels hit rough roads. Jimmy V had been driving this bus for years, but even his skill wouldn't get a bus through eighteen inches of snow. So what had Steve lined up that would?

The man watched his phone, then popped onto his feet. The bus shifted, taking another turn. Instead of accelerating afterward, the vehicle parked. Steve led the way out, Gannon and Tim right behind him. Nicole and John fell into the middle of the lineup. Philip and his family brought up the rear.

They stepped onto the slushy pavement of a well-lit lot. Streetlights illuminated an industrial building with five garage doors, each painted with a familiar logo.

"Jacked and Twisted." Gannon clapped a hand on Steve's shoulder, his voice full of wonder and laughter, like a kid who'd opened his favorite gaming system on Christmas morning.

Three men exited the building with a small camera crew trailing.

Nicole leaned against John's arm, holding her thin trench coat shut against the cold. "What is this place?"

John slid his arm around her to help her stay warm. He could give her the gift he'd gotten her early, before Christmas with his family, but she wouldn't have much to open as the rest of them tore into their gifts. He'd wait, trying to keep her from being too uncomfortable in the meantime. "They're a custom shop with a reality show."

"I take it you're fans."

John grinned as he led her forward to join the introductions and get that much closer to seeing what a place like this, known for their extreme trucks, would send them off in.

The shop's owner launched into a speech that seemed as much for their benefit as for the benefit of the cameras. "You guys lucked out. We're here wrapping up a job tonight. Christmas present for Granite Thompson from his wife."

John caught Nicole's questioning look. She wasn't into sports any more than she appreciated car shows. "Pro wrestler."

The owner motioned for the band to follow him.

The interior of the shop was as big and clean as it appeared on TV. The owner cut across the space toward a trio of trucks, parked at angles for effect.

"We're big Awestruck fans around here," the man continued, "so when we heard you were in a lurch, we had to help. Christmas with the people important to us, that's huge." Despite sounding scripted, he looked sincere enough as he gave Philip, who carried his sleeping son, a nod. "We have two project vehicles that are far enough along to loan out. As you can see, they won't have clearance problems unless you find snow deeper than twelve inches."

"And if we do?" John hated to push back, but the forecast called for more accumulation than that.

"They'll be fine, right?"

John understood the assurance in Gannon's voice. The SUVs appeared capable of besting anything nature threw at them. They'd been outfitted with aggressive tires. Embodying the shop's name, they'd also been jacked up, so the bumpers were waist-height.

The head mechanic bent and pointed to the chassis of the closest truck. "If the snow's deeper than a foot, you'll drag. For a short burst, that's fine, but over time, it'll get bogged down."

Gannon tipped his head, eyes focused under the truck. Finally, he shrugged. "Forecasts are wrong all the time. Besides, I'm sure they don't let roads get that buried."

Tim narrowed his eyes. "Maybe just for fun you should tell us what to do in worst-case scenarios."

Steve stepped into the circle. "Including how to pull someone out of a ditch. Just in case."

After the mechanic walked them through the instructions, the owner talked up the first vehicle to Philip and his family. The TVs built into the back of the headrests would entertain the kids when they woke.

All the while, Gannon didn't move far from the bumper of the second SUV, claiming the heavily modified black luxury vehicle, though probably unaware he was doing so.

John's interest wandered to the third option. Though an

older model and rusty around the edges, this one had been lifted and paired with a set of wheels like the others.

The owner appeared at his side. "With nine of you going on this trip, technically, you'd only need the two. But we weren't sure how light you were traveling or if you might need a third so ... This one's my son's. Not the prettiest puppy in the window, but she runs great. I trust her with my kid, after all. So, it's up to you guys."

This one looked like the most fun to John. A little more rough-and-tumble, a little less risk of scratching up a pricy paint job. He'd seen the episode where the crew found and fixed it up. They'd spared costs on the appearance because of the young driver, but the parts under the rusty exterior were solid.

"Are you sure he wants to part with it?" Gannon asked.

"For you guys, for a couple of days? Absolutely."

The weight of attention settled on John. This was his decision, because Gannon and Philip had their rides already.

If he took it, he'd spend all night and half of tomorrow alone in a vehicle with Nicole, nothing to do but talk. To fill that much time, surely Nicole would tell him about her cards and her agency. They'd clear the air in plenty of time to enjoy Christmas.

"Let's do this."

4

The rearview mirror gave Philip shadowy impressions of the kids and Joan. Nason slept in the farthest row back, and Nila had zonked out against her pillow in the seat directly behind Philip. In the bucket seat next to her, Joan also dozed. She wouldn't want to drive this SUV in this weather anyway.

"How long are you good for?" Philip's dad asked from the front passenger seat.

"Two or three hours." With the snow, keeping the vehicle on the road would take intense concentration. After being awake all day and pouring energy into the show, Philip couldn't promise much more than that without risking his family's safety. He spared a glance away from the rusty white tailgate of John's ride about five car-lengths ahead. "You can get some sleep."

Surely corralling the kids all day had taken a toll. Instead of relaxing, Dad leaned toward the radio. "Something tells me this music won't keep you awake."

"It's fine." Since he doubted any of the music he stored on his phone would help the kids sleep or meet with Joan's approval, Philip streamed an easy-listening Christian station, though he'd never been much of a fan. The answers these songs touted didn't satisfy the questions that haunted him.

Where was the love of God when Clare died? How was Philip supposed to take care of Nason and Nila without her?

Gannon's faith drove a lot of Awestruck's lyrics too, but Awestruck wasn't a Christian band. Even as an outspoken believer, the lead singer sometimes left songs at an unanswered cry for help.

Now, that was the kind of relationship with God Philip could relate to.

"So, how are you doing?"

Philip's attention shot to his father.

That silly Christmas light necklace cast bursts of color across an expression more serious than festive. Back when Philip moved the kids from Iowa back to LA, Dad's expression mirrored this one. He'd not said much, but one remark stuck with Philip. "Be the man your kids deserve."

"I'm good, Dad. Awestruck's good to me. The tour's been a whirlwind, but the good kind."

"So you're saying it's good?"

Philip smiled at the tease in his dad's voice, but the levity proved short-lived.

"And now that it's ending?" Dad prodded.

And now that it was ending, he was considering giving up his children.

Except, he couldn't admit to his own father that he himself wasn't cut out for fatherhood. He'd do what he had to. He'd fake it. Somehow, they'd get through.

"Your back has been bothering you?"

Philip struggled against a powerful impulse to squirm in his seat like a kid with a guilty conscience. "No. Pain free."

He attempted to vanquish the guilt. Since joining

Awestruck, he'd been on the straight and narrow. One more reason he could take the kids, be their father.

"Daddy?" Nila's voice stabbed the quiet.

Philip checked the mirror. "What's wrong?"

"I had a dream you weren't here." Her voice trembled, teary.

"We get to be together for Christmas. I'm going to show you the new house where we're all going to live together in a few weeks."

The house was an hour and a half from the cabin. They'd make the trip on Christmas Day, while Gannon and John visited their families.

"What if I don't like it?" Her voice wobbled, the tears increasingly evident.

He tried reassuring her, but within a half mile, her crying woke Joan. After trying to calm her unsuccessfully, Joan suggested he give his dad the wheel and move back to sit with his daughter.

Ahead of them, John's vehicle continued to lead the way down the dark highway. The precipitation fell faster than it had in the city, and a veneer of snow crystalized over the slush. He hated to ask the guys to pull over for his sake when they hadn't even been on the road an hour, but Nila's crying continued.

He used voice commands to text the others. At the next exit, they found a gas station. The other two vehicles idled as Philip, Joan, and Dad all switched seats. No sooner had Philip sat in the seat Joan vacated than Nila complained he was still too far away.

He lay his arm across the narrow space between them. Her tiny fingers gripped him, her hand completely swallowed by his. With her other hand, she held her locket, which contained a picture of Clare.

She held onto both her parents as tightly as possible, but Clare was long gone, and though present, Philip doubted his ability to serve his daughter much better.

~

ADELINE BLINKED AWAY the shadows and straightened the arm she'd been sleeping on, lifting herself to survey the room. Light from the Christmas tree fell softly on the chairs, tables, and thick rugs. Tegan's form lay cuddled under a quilt, only her blond head visible. Bruce's snoring sounded from the floor, so the glitter of eyes from Tegan's couch must have been those of one of John's dogs.

A warm, heavy weight pressed on Adeline's own legs. Sure enough, the other pit bull snuggled between her legs and the back of the couch, his massive head resting on her feet.

She sort of remembered waking when Trigger hopped up toward the end of the movie.

Now the TV was black. Auto shut-off? Or had Tegan done that? She hadn't meant to fall asleep out here. What time was it, anyway?

Adeline patted the end table until she found her phone. Three thirty.

Depending on the weather, the route they'd chosen, and when they'd actually gotten on the road, the guys could be anywhere from Milwaukee to Madison. Or near Oshkosh? She unlocked her phone, hoping Gannon would've silenced his if he were sleeping.

You up? How's it going?

Trigger sighed heavily. Adeline scratched the dog's smooth, short fur.

Her phone lit up with a reply. *Good. We're somewhere between Portage and Stevens Point.*

She researched the routes. Driving from Chicago in good weather, reaching a city as far up and over as Portage should've taken three hours. Stevens Point, four. Awestruck hadn't left Chicago until midnight, so either way, they'd made good time. Maybe too good.

You'd better be closer to Portage. Precious cargo.

She sent the text and rose, smirking. He'd never let her get away with calling him precious.

The dogs followed her from the room. Since they'd been shut in the cabin since seven thirty or eight, she let them out. The snow blanketing the property nearly reached the dogs' bellies. They did their business quickly and trotted back in, shaking off clinging flakes.

She checked her phone. No reply from Gannon.

Back in the den, Tegan remained asleep. Since she seemed comfortable, Adeline opted not to wake her.

The dogs shadowed her to the bedroom. No sooner had she pulled the covers over her legs than Camo and Trigger sprang up and plopped next to her.

"You are so spoiled."

Camo blinked at her. Trigger settled his head against the blankets.

Tired of being alone, she didn't have the heart to shoo them off.

She checked her phone. Still no word from Gannon.

He'd probably drifted off after his first reply. She ought to do the same—sleep so she'd be more rested to spend quality time together once he arrived.

Lonely impatience loomed in the darkness, nudging her awake each time her mind began to settle. Would they ever really share their lives?

Tegan had been wise to suggest she seek remote career opportunities.

She might sleep better with a possible solution in mind, so she ran a job search.

Most of the results seemed to be customer service representatives. She could only imagine what it'd be like to take shifts on the phone, answering questions about cable channels or hiking boots from some hotel while the band ran a sound check.

Sighing, she slid the phone onto the nightstand and pulled the blankets up to her chin. She wasn't alone. God was with her, and Gannon would be soon. People endured far more heart-wrenching separations than a rock star and his girlfriend.

But knowing the facts didn't lend her peace.

Because peace came from God, not knowledge. Hadn't she learned that by now? Instead of another fruitless job search, she turned to prayer, and somewhere in that, found sleep.

~

NICOLE'S CRY pulled John out of a dream.

Snow pelted the windows. The seatbelt banded tight on his chest as the vehicle skidded. An ominous shadow passed out the window. The truck came to a stop, askew in the far-right lane of the interstate.

John twisted. No traffic besides Philip's SUV, which passed in the next lane, then pulled over. The shadow they'd passed was the third truck, the one Tim drove, pointed the wrong direction.

"Pull onto the shoulder," John instructed.

When they'd last stopped, at three a.m., John and Gannon had realized they needed to put their Californians at the wheel —in fact, they should've let the inexperienced winter drivers have the first shift. That way, John and Gannon could rest and be ready to take back over when conditions got worse.

Which, apparently, they had.

"Did you see that?" Nicole placed both hands on the wheel and sat as tall as possible, as if seeing the road right before her would help her steer onto the shoulder. "One second they were there, and the next..." She circled her hand through the air as if

Tim fell victim to a tornado. "Are we going to have to tow them?"

"We'll see." He dipped his head, watching in the mirror. They weren't in deep. The truck's four-wheel drive ought to get them out.

John's phone buzzed with a message from Gannon.

At least our warm-weather friends made it three hours.

John chuckled.

"What's funny?" Nicole asked.

John shook off his smile. "They're all right. Tim's not used to winter driving."

A group text from Philip arrived. *Kids woke up. Need a pit stop.*

Behind them, Tim and Gannon's SUV rolled forward and back, still stuck.

Gannon sent a message to the group. *Wausau's a couple minutes ahead. We'll stop at the first gas station.*

Tim's engine revved, and the SUV broke free into the lane. Gannon must plan to wait for the stop to switch places with Tim. Not the worst idea. In this, other drivers wouldn't see vehicles stopped on the edge of the highway until they were right on top of them, making this a dangerous place to get out.

John looked to Nicole. "Are you okay until Wausau?"

"Yeah." Nicole shifted back into gear. "I don't understand how Tim spun around like that. Aren't these supposed to drive through anything? Everything's been going fine."

"Be careful. It doesn't take much." From the looks of it, no plows had been through in hours. Hopefully, crews were making the rounds though. So far, their caravan remained on track to reach their destination around ten a.m., but if conditions deteriorated, their remaining four hours could stretch much longer.

Tim retook the lead, followed by Philip. Nicole pressed the

accelerator to fall in line, and snow flew up from the tires past the windows. The truck edged sideways instead of advancing.

"Slow and steady," John said. Though given her enthusiasm for the gas pedal, she'd be a lot of fun in an empty, snow-covered parking lot.

In the relative quiet, once they reached speed, John noticed the music.

"You're playing Awestruck?"

"Of course." She flashed him her best smile. "I love your music."

Awestruck had plenty of fans, but praise from someone he cared about? The simple compliment slipped past his defenses. Nicole hadn't explained herself yet, but he'd slept the last couple of hours, and they still had hours to go.

"So that gift Gannon spent all day shopping for. Guess what he got her." Nicole's tone said she wouldn't suppress the secret long, so he waited until she supplied the answer. "A tree growing kit. Is Adeline really into trees or something?"

"No." The last time John saw her property, the only plant he'd spotted inside or out was the grass in the lawn. "I'm sure he has his reasons."

"It's cute that he tried that hard and that's the best he could do." Nicole laughed with a shake of her head. "The basses will save him if she likes playing as much as you say."

Fair enough. Music constituted an important part of Gannon and Adeline's bond, but even a spot-on present wasn't what the couple needed most. "The best gift for them is the tour ending."

Nicole spared him a smile. "It's nice that our traveling hasn't been such a strain for us. Some of my exes minded my schedule, and eventually, you can't enjoy the time you do have together. But we free each other to follow our dreams, and when we're together, we get to do things like this."

"You like this?"

"My friends are going to be very impressed I managed to drive a massive truck through a blizzard." She scrunched her nose, grinning. "I bet none of them suspect I have it in me, and I hate being underestimated."

Understandable. Was he underestimating her regarding her financial situation? Possibly, and by asking about it, he'd reveal that low opinion to her. Instead, he'd give her more time to broach the subject herself.

For now, she remained cheerfully focused on their trip. "The whole cabin thing is very quaint and sweet, and I'm looking forward to meeting your family. I've been studying. Want to quiz me?"

"On what?"

"Your family."

"You studied my family?"

She'd asked for names a while ago, but he hadn't thought much of it.

"Of course. Your parents are Hank and Patricia—although Hank is your stepdad. Your real dad has been out of the picture since you were a kid."

A kid, but old enough to remember, unfortunately. Nic had pressed for the story earlier in their relationship and seemed hurt when he'd resisted sharing.

Telling her now would deepen their relationship, but the details froze in his throat.

She plowed onward, describing his family. "Your sisters are Kate, Stacy, and Angie. Ask me the names of their husbands."

He watched her sitting proudly behind the wheel, eyes scanning the snow. "What are their husbands' names?"

"That's a trick question. Kate is only engaged, not married. Tanner is her fiancé. Angie is married to Mark. Stacy to Rob."

"Robby."

She narrowed her eyes, smirking. "If that's the worst you can say, I'm doing pretty well."

She was. He was impressed, but there was another quality he liked about her: she could take a little ribbing.

"You've been internet stalking."

"Researching. This is important. I want to get it right. Make a good first impression."

"You always do." Since her beautiful face invariably made up the first impression she gave. Beyond that, she was thoughtful and adventurous. He'd never doubted she'd made him a priority, arranging her schedule to see him, willingly taking part in plans like this one.

"Well, now you know my secret."

"Research."

A shrug. A nod.

Putting extra effort into relationships came naturally to her. Yet another reason theirs worked. Another reason to start sharing more and building a more solid relationship.

He took the simplest first step. "While we're up north, I'm checking out a house. Come with me?"

She shot him a million-dollar smile. "I'd love to."

They weren't Adeline and Gannon. John and Nicole didn't have that much history, and maybe that was a good thing, since Gannon and Adeline had spent years recovering from their past. And John's house wouldn't be a shared decision the way Gannon's had been. He and Nicole weren't that far along in their relationship.

But if Gannon and Adeline could get past all the bumps to their own happily-ever-after, John and Nicole might too.

5

*T*he gas station attendant was staring. Or, at least, she had been when Gannon looked directly at her—something he wouldn't normally have done, but she'd drawn his attention, thanks to her headband with felt antlers and little bells.

Realizing he'd made a mistake that could get him recognized, he'd taken cover by the carafes of coffee. Usually, he was game for autographs when someone asked, but some fans wanted more than an autograph. They wanted pictures and conversation and for him to wait until their friends made it over to see him too.

That was a lot to deal with before seven in the morning, when all he wanted was to get to Adeline.

When footsteps advanced toward him, he resisted turning. A certain level of shy fan would leave him alone if he acted oblivious.

An elbow bumped his arm. "Now that would be a coffee cup."

No wonder he hadn't heard the jingle of the headband. The

"fan" was John, not the antler-toting employee. He pointed to the stacks of fifty-ounce plastic cups next to the carafes.

Gannon took a medium paper cup from the other side. "Next time we give Tim the overnight shift at the wheel, we'll have to make sure he has one filled to the brim."

John took two large coffee cups, apparently shopping for Nicole too, while he waited for Gannon to finish. "He fell asleep?"

"All I know for sure is that I did. I woke up, and we were on the shoulder already. Hard to get a straight answer out of him. Either he fell asleep, or he was texting." The heat of the coffee warmed the paper as the level rose. He grabbed a travel sleeve and stepped out of John's way. "Or he doesn't want to admit a little snow got the better of him."

"More than a little."

Before Gannon could concede the point, a screech turned both of their heads toward the hall with the bathrooms.

"You're too old for the men's bathroom, Nila." The stern frustration in Philip's voice carried around the corner. "Go with Grandma. You're a big girl now."

Though loud, Nila's blubbering reply was incoherent. Gannon and John shared a look. Was that what fatherhood was going to be like? Begging compliance from ornery kids when he was hardly upright himself?

The intervention in the hall continued. "I'm not going to leave you here," Philip said. "And I'd never forget you."

More blubbering, despite the tenderness of Philip's assurances.

John blew out a breath. "Dogs don't like changes to their routine either."

"Somehow, I doubt it's the same."

"Fair enough." John fit the lids on his coffee cups and headed toward the register.

Over the metallic garland topping the shelving unit,

Gannon spotted Tim in the candy aisle. Their manager watched the exchange in the hallway for a moment, then returned his focus to the shelves before him. He didn't talk about his daughter much. Did seeing Philip with his kids make Tim jealous, sad, or relieved?

Gannon doctored his coffee with two pumps of hazelnut syrup and joined Tim in the snack aisle. The manager had collected two candy bars, two reindeer-shaped jelly bean dispensers, and three bananas.

"Puppy chow?" Gannon hit his finger against the corner of the bag that topped the collection. "I thought you were going to sleep."

Tim made a face and re-examined the bag, which contained rice cereal coated in chocolate, peanut butter, and powdered sugar. "This isn't for dogs. It has chocolate in it."

"No, that's what it's called. Puppy chow."

The packaging crinkled as Tim flashed the name at Gannon. "Not officially."

Gannon held up his hands, surrendering the point. "Why all the sugar? We only have three hours to go."

"In this weather?"

Touché. "There will be other gas stations."

"I want this stuff now. When'd you get judgy?"

Gannon snorted. "If you end up with a sugar high, I'm deporting you to Philip's truck with the other kids."

"You do that." Tim headed for one of the beverage coolers.

Gannon took his coffee, a cinnamon muffin, and an apple to the checkout. He set the purchases on the counter and kept his eyes trained on the newspapers as he got out his wallet.

"Are you Gannon Vaughn?"

Busted. If not for *Audition Room*, the reality show he used to judge, he may have escaped without her being sure enough to ask. After all, John had paid for his coffee without being recognized while Gannon was in the snack aisle.

He put a ten on the counter, since his credit card would've sealed the deal. "If I were, would I be driving around up here in this weather on Christmas Eve?"

"If Gannon Vaughn drove around up here in this weather"—the clerk's headband jingled as she nodded out the window at the blacked-out, lifted SUV—"*that's* exactly what I'd expect."

"Quit holding up the line." Tim's voice, loaded with the fake annoyance of a sarcastic complaint, came from directly over his shoulder.

"I'm doing my best here." Fighting a laugh, Gannon pushed his ten toward the clerk.

She watched him as she made his change, not once looking at her till. She blindly—but still correctly—counted his change back to him.

"All right." A chuckled escaped. "It's Christmas. What can I sign for you?"

"I knew it!"

Tim dumped his load of snacks, now rounded out by three bottles of juice and a few candy canes, onto the counter as the cashier grabbed for paper.

She slid it to Gannon, grinning.

He read the tag on her shirt. "Kendra?"

She nodded eagerly, the felt antlers quivering.

"All right. But take care of him"—Gannon tipped the end of the pen toward Tim—"or he'll make that tantrum in the hall look like a walk in the park."

Tim smiled innocently as the cashier quickly scanned his items.

She gave Tim his total as Gannon finished the autograph.

Tim stuck his card in the reader, and she focused on Gannon again before he could step away. "Any chance I can get a picture with you? My friends will never believe this."

He wanted to get on the road, but he forced a kind smile and motioned her out from behind the counter.

By the time she'd finished Tim's transaction and removed the antlers, Philip and his kids exited the bathrooms. Gannon called him over to join the shot, and the kids waited nearby with their grandparents. Tim took the cashier's phone and stepped back to snap the picture.

John must've seen the interaction from his truck, because as Tim finished the countdown for the picture, the drummer stepped back in. Somehow, after a few more pictures and autographs, John was also the first to head back outside.

With one final *Merry Christmas*, Gannon reached the door in time to catch it for Philip and his kids. Red rimmed Nila's big eyes, and Nason's cowlick covered about half of his head. Philip looked little better.

"Anything I can do to help?" Gannon asked.

Philip shook his head as he ushered the kids past and into the air lock. Snow peppered the glass of the small enclosure. It was a dismal day when a gas station made a more comfortable environment than the outdoors.

"Hang on a minute." Tim took advantage of the door Gannon still held and knelt, setting the less-full of his two shopping bags behind him, and holding the other toward the kids. Candy and juice bulged against the plastic. "You guys won't believe what happened."

Nason rubbed an eye.

Nila gripped her locket and looked from Tim to her dad, who'd hesitated instead of opening the exterior door, looking as skeptically interested as his kids.

"The cashier said that, right before we got here, she saw something flying in the sky." Tim used a storytelling inflection Gannon had never heard from him before. "Do you know what it was?"

Nason shook his head.

Nila bit her lip.

"It might've been a sleigh. It's Christmas Eve, you know."

Her lip still clamped between her teeth, Nila glanced up at her dad, dimples forming in her cheeks.

"They said this fell out." Tim extended the bag closer. "They found it in the parking lot with a note saying to give it to two kids they'd see this morning. Do you think that might be you?"

Nason pulled the lip of the bag toward himself and peered inside. His eyes got about as big as the tires on the trucks out in the lot.

Nila moved in too.

Tim sat back on his heels. "I can only give this to you if you promise to not fight about it."

Nila's lip came unstuck. "I promise."

Nason echoed her.

"Okay. Don't drop it." Tim released the bag to her. "And wait until you're back in the car to open anything."

"Promise," she said.

Tim straightened again to get the exterior door.

Squinting against the pelting snow, Gannon fell in step beside him as Philip and the kids jogged ahead. "I didn't think you had it in you."

"What? A heart?"

"That, and stories about Santa."

Tim yanked open the passenger door of their SUV. "I've been Santa Claus to Awestruck on more than one occasion."

Gannon climbed behind the wheel and slammed the door, tilting his head to keep the snow that blew in from reaching his neck.

"When you see the zeroes on your next contract, you can start calling me Saint Nick."

"I don't think that's how sainthood works."

"What do you call a guy who takes a chance on a band with

terrible clothes, one radio-ready song, and a lead singer known for launching into sermons mid-show?"

"An optimist." Chuckling, Gannon looked down the line of vehicles. Philip's folks were still in the store, the last of the group to return. "The risk worked out for you, didn't it?"

As if to cover a smile, Tim lifted the bottle of juice he hadn't handed off to the kids. "Don't get cocky."

"Whatever you say, Saint Nick."

∼

THE TRUCK IDLED while John and Nicole waited for Philip's parents to finish inside. Despite the blowers running full blast, Nicole curled her hands around her cup of coffee.

"You look cold."

"I am cold. It's like ... It's so cold, it seeps through and settles in your bones." Despite her serious tone, John struggled not to smile. Temperatures hovered in the twenties. Wisconsin could do about fifty degrees worse without breaking any records.

"A nice coat helps." He eyed her designer trench again and checked on Philip's parents.

Still at the register. John put his coffee in the cupholder and reached into the backseat. It took both hands to produce the wrapped rectangular box he'd personally moved from the bus to the truck.

Nicole slid her coffee into the cupholder next to his. "I get to open a present? Now?"

He nodded. No reason she needed to be uncomfortable all day when he had a solution with him, even if giving the gift now meant she'd have nothing to open at his parents' house.

She tore the silver-and-gold gift wrap with a giddy laugh. Within about twenty seconds, she held the winter coat he'd picked for her. Thick and hip-length, the layer was rated to thirty below. She liked to wear white, and the belt ought to slim down the bulky garment.

"So you won't be cold every time you come up to see me."

"That's thoughtful." She smoothed her hands over the surface of the coat but didn't make a move to slide her arms into the sleeves.

"It's warm." The same brand as his own coat. Not the posh designers she usually wore, but high quality.

"Thank you." She lay it over her lap like a blanket and picked her coffee up with a twitch of a smile.

She didn't like it.

"I know it's not a fancy label."

"It's nice. Warm." She shifted in her seat, as if snuggling in. "I only got you one gift, or I'd give you one of my small ones now too."

Small ones?

Sure, the coat cost less than the bracelet. And yes, he bought her a nicer gift that she hadn't discovered yet. So why did her assumption that he'd gotten her more rub him the wrong way?

Because of the question about her finances. After over six hours in the car, she still hadn't explained.

She must've read the offense on his face, because her expression fell. "I'm sorry. This is really nice. It's okay if it's all you got me. I like it. It'll be warm."

Yeah, especially if she'd put it on. But he didn't tell her to because, if she did, she might find the other part of the present, and he didn't want her to have that right now.

"John." She rested her hand on his forearm. "This is a good gift. Thank you."

He nodded, but he couldn't force himself to reply.

Philip's parents finally exited the store and got into their vehicle, so John shifted into reverse.

"It's just that I spent more. That's all. I thought we were getting to a certain level."

Now out of the stall, he jolted the shifter into drive. "What level?"

"I ... Never mind. I'm sorry. This is really great. I appreciate you making sure I'm warm."

As she should. What level did she estimate their relationship might be on that he wouldn't be concerned about her comfort?

As the trio of trucks resumed their trek, their speed, combined with the wind and snow, hampered visibility. The risen sun only illuminated more of the shapeless white around them.

"You're angry."

Oh, how he was.

She had no right to harbor expectations for how much he'd spend on her when she'd supplied so many reasons to doubt how responsibly she handled her own resources.

They'd been on the road since midnight. Clearly, she wouldn't volunteer the information he wanted. He'd have to ask, but if he did so now, his anger would come through, so he chose silence instead.

~

THE SUV's engine was loud, but not loud enough to block Nila's whining. "But Santa wanted us to have the candy."

"And Jesus wants you to obey your grandparents," Joan returned.

Philip's dad smiled in the passenger seat.

Philip rubbed his forehead. "Listen to Grandma, Nila."

She sniffed but quit fighting for the goodies from Tim and accepted the banana instead. As she and Nason ate, they focused on the children's movie Joan dug out of the luggage.

Not long after they'd finished the bananas, both kids succumbed to sleep again.

Small mercies.

The roads weren't great, but Philip had learned to drive in his own truck in Iowa, where snow and gravel roads had prepared him for this. As long as they kept going in straight lines through less than five inches of snow, they'd be all right. Unless Gannon let Tim drive again.

Philip checked the mirror to make sure the kids were still out and lowered his voice. He shouldn't have to ask this, but he'd rather know than guess wrong. "They don't still believe in Santa, do they?"

"They'd believe just about anything they think would get them candy," Joan said wryly.

Dad chuckled.

Philip glanced over. That hadn't been an answer.

Dad sipped his coffee and shook his head. Sometime in the night, the batteries on the lighted necklace had gone out. "They don't."

Good, because they had enough going against them without him having to burst that bubble too.

6

*A*deline took one last slurp from her coffee mug before pulling on gloves. The end of Bruce's six-foot leash disappeared around the corner as the dog sprinted to the front door. Camo and Trigger, who sat patiently waiting for her, wore much longer lead lines attached to their collars because their calmer demeanors meant they were less likely to venture into trouble when they headed out in a minute.

Bruce trotted back in, barked once as if to tell her to hurry, and took another lap.

She ought to see if John's dog trainer could do a few sessions with her lab.

"Or maybe you don't like the coats. Is that why you're sitting so still?" She looked from one pit bull to the other. Because of their short fur, she'd buttoned them into the insulated, water-proof vests she'd found among their supplies.

Tegan tromped into the room, her orange snow pants clashing with her fuchsia coat.

Not that the second pair of orange pants, which they'd found in a closet, looked much better with Adeline's powder blue jacket. Judging by the scene out the window, they'd soon be grateful for both the high visibility orange and the added warmth.

Adeline settled her hat over the tops of her ears. "You'd tell me if this were a bad idea, right?"

"It's coming down, but it's not a whiteout, and it's warm enough. Following the road will be easy enough. We'll be fine."

"Okay. Let's see how far we make it." Adeline caught Bruce's leash before he made another lap and left the easier two to Tegan.

Outside, the snow continued, but the woods calmed the wind to reasonable breezes. At least a foot had accumulated, leaving the dogs to jump through while Adeline and Tegan high-stepped. By the time they'd ventured one hundred yards from the cabin, Adeline unzipped the top half of her coat to cool off.

This hike was a reconnaissance mission. No one had cleared the private drive to the cabin since the start of the storm. That drive was only about a quarter mile, so the guys could hike from the turn off if they couldn't get their trucks through. If, however, the plows hadn't reached the country highway leading to the driveway, they'd have a problem. The SUVs couldn't overcome miles and miles of foot-deep snow, especially when the flakes piled higher every minute.

Camo plunged into a drift and sprang up like a boat fighting white caps. Bruce paused to wag his tail as he watched his buddy. Before the older dog got any ideas, Adeline guided him around the deeper section. Meanwhile, Trigger wisely followed Bruce, leveraging the lab's trampled path.

"It is pretty." The effort to wade the drifts turned Tegan breathless.

Adeline lifted her gaze. Snowy pines crowded the private drive on either side until the falling snow obscured the view in the middle distance. The dogs, now fanned out over the road, peered back at the humans they would otherwise outpace. She dug out her phone, slipped off a glove, and snapped a picture.

She attached the image to a text to Gannon and John. *Wish you were here.*

She plodded on, sweating beneath her layers. Last night's wind had left two thigh-high drifts on the private drive. Trigger and Camo seemed to have unlimited energy, but Adeline observed Bruce, ready to turn around if he seemed to tire.

Finally, they approached the main road. The layer of snow on the main road stood even with that on the cabin's private drive.

"Not plowed," Tegan said.

"Not once." Adeline trudged to the edge of the T-shaped intersection and peered both directions. Pure white as far as the eye could see. She took out her phone and captured another picture to send to the guys.

When she opened the group conversation, two replies waited in response to her earlier message about wishing the guys were already at the cabin.

Gannon's first: *Working on it.*

John had sent a GIF of a monster truck climbing a snowbank.

Her gaze tracked back to Gannon's response. First, he'd suddenly stopped replying last night, and now he sounded almost annoyed. He must be tired.

That would be understandable.

But if he was going to be exhausted all Christmas because of this overnight push to get to the cabin, it'd be Thanksgiving all over again.

They might've been better off canceling.

"What?" Tegan asked.

Adeline shook her head and composed her text. *The main road hasn't been plowed.*

She attached the picture and hit send, and they tugged the leashes and turned back for the cabin.

~

WHEN ANOTHER TEXT CAME IN, Nicole held John's phone out to him. He glanced at the screen long enough to confirm the new arrival came from Adeline, then put his finger over the sensor.

With the phone unlocked, Nicole read off the text. "She says the main road hasn't been plowed."

"We won't reach that road for over an hour." They moved steadily but couldn't travel at the speed limit without risking losing control. At this rate, the plows might have two or three hours to visit the road before they arrived at the juncture.

"Is that what you want me to say to her?"

He tapped his thumbs on the steering wheel, keeping beat with the classic rock they'd found on the radio. "Find an unstoppable GIF."

Nicole scrolled through some search results, laughed, and turned the phone again.

He glanced over but only got an impression of two dark figures and text at the bottom. He refocused on the road and keeping all four tires on it. "Can't see."

"It's two Celtic warriors or something, and the subtitle is, 'Nothing can stop us.' There's even snow in the background."

"Perfect."

She returned to work. "Oh. Another message. This one's about the house. The real estate agent says she can make it despite the storm if you can."

John checked the clock on the dash. "Tell her if we can't, I'll give her an hour warning. And thank her for making time on Christmas Eve."

Nicole typed on the device, and he assumed she was transcribing the message, but a moment later, she said, "This is the house?"

She must've found the link to the listing in his message history. By her tone, what she saw didn't impress her.

Hadn't he known that would be the case?

"What do you like about it?"

"All the land." The answer was true, but incomplete. Something about the house reminded him of his childhood home, despite the differences between the two. Both seemed equally lived in, practical, and comfortable.

Like a home.

Would Nic understand that?

She bent closer to the screen. "A lot of square footage, I guess. I suppose you can fix it up however you want. The wood paneling's got to go. But ... With your budget, why buy a bargain property?"

The asking amount was pretty hefty to call a bargain. "I don't mind paying fair market price for a well-cared-for property with fifty acres of woods."

"Even if you end up remodeling the whole thing?"

He shrugged. He would do updates if he bought the place. Potentially extensive ones, but he would also preserve some of the original character.

A few taps later, she set the phone on the seat.

He didn't want to talk, but the longer he put this off, the worse his resentment grew.

His fingers kept beat with a new song on the radio. "Did you research us too?"

"Us?"

"The band. Before you came to a show."

She'd researched his family after he'd invited her on this trip, and she'd said she liked to be prepared. How much prep work had she completed between meeting him at the taping and showing up backstage at that Awestruck show?

"Sure, I looked a few things up. Like any good fan. And it was a lot easier than your family. There's a ton about you guys out there. Gannon especially, but I've always thought drummers are intriguing. Back there, the heartbeat of the band while he lets someone else have the spotlight."

The heartbeat of the band. He liked that, even if he hated the rest of it. "What did you learn?" He added a smile for good measure.

"Oh, the big stuff. That you were high school pals—you and Gannon. That Philip's a dad. References to your guys' faith were hard to miss."

"I didn't think we'd make a supermodel so curious." He'd considered the playing field pretty even when they'd met, both supporting a non-profit, both famous, both well-paid.

She unbuckled and slid into the middle of the bench seat to interlace her fingers with his. "I didn't attend your show as a supermodel. I attended as a fan. And you guys might try to bury it under tattoos and monster trucks, but you're good guys, and good guys are hard to find." She chuckled. "Especially rich ones."

Was she serious? Had he misheard? "Rich ones?"

She shrugged. "Say what you want, but money matters. I've dated guys who make less than I do, and it always becomes a thing. Better to find someone who isn't threatened by my income." She squeezed his hand and stretched to kiss his cheek before settling in and buckling the seatbelt. "You and I are evenly matched. One more reason we work so well."

"Except we're not. I make more." By a longshot.

Nicole laughed. "You're also humble."

If she had a guilty conscience about money, she wouldn't seem so carefree, would she?

If his suspicions were wrong, of course she'd said nothing about the declined cards and the meeting with her agency. But money mattered to her, or she wouldn't have emphasized his income. She wouldn't have turned up her nose at the coat.

Right?

Pushing for answers would risk the relationship. He didn't want to do that at Christmas. But he also couldn't let this go and enjoy the holiday.

He stilled his drumming. The road seemed to stretch forever, an endless tunnel that may or may not get them where they wanted to go.

He needed advice. An unbiased opinion. "Can you text the others that I need to stop?"

"Too much coffee?" She used her own phone to send the message, and a minute later read the responses. "Philip says the kids needed a stop anyway."

A few minutes later, Gannon pulled off the road and into the lot of a gas station that boasted only two pumps.

The other two pulled up first, so John idled behind Gannon's SUV. "I can take it from here, if you want to go in."

"Are you sure? Didn't you need a break?"

"I'm fine."

She slipped from the cab and tightened her trench around herself as she jogged past the other trucks. Her hair whipped in the breeze as she looked both ways before crossing the aisle between the pumps and the store. He grabbed the coat she hadn't put on and tossed it in the back seat. Once she disappeared inside, he left the warmth of the truck.

Gannon hopped as if to keep warm while fuel pumped into his vehicle. John shoved his hands in his pockets and stood where the black SUV would shield him from the snowy breeze.

Gannon stilled. "What's wrong?"

"Nic. I think her credit cards are maxed out."

Gannon's expression registered no surprise. So he'd come to the same conclusion, probably all the way back at the mall.

Why hadn't John acted on his suspicions then? Or even

further back? At Thanksgiving, he could've pushed harder about her debt.

He hadn't because he hadn't wanted to derail this. Not ever, but especially not right before Christmas.

And yet, did he still have a choice?

"Her agency called her unreliable. Said she's been skipping gigs." Saying it aloud cemented it. He'd been a fool to choose denial and silence so long.

Gannon studied him for a few long beats, stray snowflakes blowing under the carport and swirling between them. "So she's got money problems she's not real intent on fixing."

John was sliding down a hill of ice toward a truth even worse than dishonesty and irresponsibility. What if she was in this relationship only for his bank account? Since they were only together a couple of days at a time, maintaining any number of lies wouldn't be that hard.

The pump thumped as the tank finished filling, but Gannon stayed focused on John. "I didn't think you two were serious."

"I invited her to Christmas."

"I wondered about that."

John frowned. This year had been full of travel and band obligations—distractions—but he'd never meant to entangle himself in a relationship to nowhere. Was that what he'd gotten himself into? Yes. Under the guise of assuming the best of her, he'd ignored problems he ought to have confronted.

"You've got to talk to her."

Talking with a liar wouldn't get him very far.

But this was Nic.

She had good qualities. They both took time out of their schedules for causes they believed in, or they wouldn't have met in the first place. She'd put energy into preparing to meet his family. She was adventurous enough to drive a jacked-up truck through a snowstorm. They'd been together the better part of a year. He wanted the relationship to work—perhaps a little too much.

"I wanted to enjoy Christmas."

Gannon's frown held understanding. Possibly pity.

Maybe they both recognized John wanted more than one holiday. He'd watched Gannon and Adeline fall in love, and he wanted a relationship of his own. A promise of family someday.

But he couldn't build a future with a woman he couldn't discuss money with.

He returned to his truck and waited for his turn to fuel up.

He'd just parked at the pump when Nic came back out. He exited and circled around the back to get to the fuel, avoiding her and her insistence on not wearing the coat. If she'd give it a chance and put it on, she'd be a lot less disappointed in the gift and in him.

But the disappointment was mutual.

Merry Christmas.

~

As HE WAITED in the gas station parking lot, Gannon inspected the pictures Adeline sent.

Jacked and Twisted warned they could plow through the occasional snowbank but that the trucks would get bogged down if the chassis dragged over long distances. They only had about a foot of clearance between the road and the axels. Judging by how high the snow in the photos rose on the dogs, the last road and the private drive were both buried deeper than that.

He backed out of the group conversation and tapped on Adeline's name, opening their one-on-one messages to update her on their progress. He would mention something about John and Nicole too, so she wouldn't be surprised if she caught on to tension at the cabin. And so she could pray.

To speak up, John must've been pretty upset.

Before typing anything new, Gannon skimmed their last messages. One from Addie about precious cargo, sent at three thirty that morning. Why hadn't he seen that?

He scrolled, reviewing the conversation.

A conversation he hadn't had. This had been during Tim's shift at the wheel.

Cold air swirled into the vehicle as the manager climbed back into his seat. "Ready to end this?"

"Were you sending texts on my phone?"

Tim's mouth popped open, and his gaze dipped to the phone. "You were sleeping. She just wanted an update."

No, she'd wanted more than that, or she wouldn't have called him precious.

No wonder Tim had been single all those years.

Tim lifted his hands in surrender. "Sorry, man. Won't happen again."

No, it wouldn't, because Gannon would change his passcode as soon as he had a few minutes to spare. He fired off a few messages to Adeline before focusing back on Tim. "The roads by the cabin haven't been plowed at all."

"Okay." Tim winced and took out his own phone. "I'll see what I can do."

The easy compliance either meant Tim was still determined to play Santa Claus, or he really did regret texting Adeline from Gannon's phone.

Gannon would take it, either way.

From the driver's seat of the next vehicle over, Philip gave him a thumbs up. In the rearview mirror, he spotted John and Nicole in the last SUV, still parked at the pump but fueled and ready.

Trusting Tim would find a solution before they reached the unplowed section, Gannon put his truck in gear and turned the wheel toward Adeline.

7

---

*T*he kids wore headphones as they watched the latest animated movie. Dad, who'd done the lion's share of the driving, slept in the middle row. Thanks to him, Philip and Joan were the best-rested adults in their entourage, so Dad had more than earned the shut-eye.

Less than fifty miles separated them from the cabin, and they drove at a good clip through the forested countryside. He guessed a plow had been through a few hours before because the snow stood only about four inches deep, and the rise of a snowbank marked the edges of the road.

That didn't mean they had it easy.

Spotting deer in the road would be nearly impossible, especially now that the muted, risen sun meant it was too bright for an animal's eyes to reflect the headlights. Even without the danger of animals, a slight miscalculation in steering could result in a skid, as evidenced by all the vehicles they'd seen awaiting tows overnight.

Joan consulted her phone. "Just three turns to go, including the one onto the property. Next left is in one and a half miles."

"Thanks." These long, straight roads seemed unending, and

knowing the next landmark added a light at the end of the tunnel.

Trees skimmed by, heavy and white. Philip realized he was squinting. Were the clouds thinning?

"I don't think I was ever as young and energetic as all of you," Joan mused.

Philip glanced from the road.

She motioned toward the windshield, where Gannon's SUV led the way. "I don't know how you're all still driving in straight lines."

"I guess we all have our skills." He rubbed his hand on the thigh of his jeans, heart pounding as he finally broached the topic that had been so heavy on his mind. "I don't know how you take care of the kids the way you do."

"Oh, you do fine. They're tired and crabby. Given a good night's rest, tomorrow will be a new day."

The simple answer did nothing to allay his concerns. "Something tells me showing them the new house won't make much of a Christmas present, given how Nila feels about moving. She's going to be begging to stay with you." He could imagine the tantrum now. If only he could grant her that wish, allow her to live with people who actually understood how to relate to and take care of her and her brother.

His throat ached, and his breath thinned. He didn't have the heart to ask, but if the kids made a big enough scene, Joan and Dad might offer.

"She loves you." Joan's tone deepened, turning serious, as if she saw through his attempt to keep this conversation casual. "There will be a transition. Remember that's only temporary."

"Until next year, when we go back on tour and she has to transition again."

Joan didn't respond.

He found her studying him. Neck burning, he put his focus back on the road.

"Long separations are always hard on families," she offered finally.

"It'd be a lot easier if you guys lived close by." He tossed it out, hoping to sound carefree, but that could be the perfect solution. He would benefit from having the kids in his life, meanwhile, the kids would have better caretakers nearby.

"Yes. It's nice being so close to my kids. It's too bad your work doesn't allow you to be in the neighborhood too."

Right. Dad and Joan couldn't up and move because of his inability to be who the kids needed him to be.

"Have you considered what you're going to do for the next tour?" she asked.

He willed himself to stay still—expression fixed, grip unchanging on the wheel, foot lightly resting on the gas—though his mind whipped into a tailspin. He'd assumed Dad and Joan would take them again.

Clearly, she didn't assume the same.

He'd thought he had a decision to make regarding his children's care, but with that sentence, Joan closed off his options. She and Dad wouldn't take the kids more. They wanted them less.

Gannon's brake lights flashed through the haze of snow, and his blinker came on.

Philip followed suit, scanning for the turn off. The ridge of snow left by the plow along the side of the road didn't seem to have a break in it.

Finally, he spotted the white-and-black sign marking the intersection. No wonder he hadn't seen an opening where the other road branched off—there wasn't one. A crew must've cleared the road they were currently driving on more recently. They'd have to break through a two-and-a-half-foot barrier of snow to take the turnoff.

Gannon turned, and the rooster tails of snow indicated he'd

gunned the throttle to get through. Joan gasped as the lead truck veered sideways, skidding half into the ditch.

"Oh, no." Joan gripped her armrest as if Philip would follow suit, but he hung back to give Gannon room to free himself.

The wheels spun, but the vehicle didn't budge. Towing him out would mean taking the turn—carefully, so they didn't hit Gannon or end up in the ditch beside him—and hoping the trucks could get enough traction in all the snow.

"You've got to turn here so you can straighten out the wheels before you hit the extra snow," Dad said from the back seat. "Hit it straight on and keep your speed slow and steady. At least he plowed off half the snow for you."

How long had Dad been awake? Long enough to overhear Philip's talk with Joan? If so, did he realize how ill-prepared Philip was to raise the kids?

As he lined up for the turn, the questions turned him as rigid as Joan looked, clinging to her seat as if she'd been strapped into a rollercoaster against her will.

The vehicle navigated the corner without incident. He pulled forward so John could follow suit. Once all the trucks were around the corner, he and his dad got out to talk strategy with the others.

As they walked around the vehicle, Philip checked Dad's expression, wondering if Dad and Joan decided together that they wouldn't take the kids again. Dad's full attention was riveted on the half-sunken vehicle.

Gannon's door opened, and he jumped down into knee-deep snow.

"You look like you need a tow," Dad called, as if he'd happened across a stranded stranger.

Gannon grinned. "Yes, sir, I think so."

"It's gonna be rough getting traction in this." Dad kicked the six or seven inches coating the roadway. The snow packed into a clump that landed a few feet away.

John descended from his truck, tow straps in hand. "Right where Jacked and Twisted said, but I've never done this."

Dad motioned for him to hand them over. "I knew you'd need me for something."

～

WHEN THE TRUCK finally pulled free of the ditch, Gannon shouted and honked the horn. Escaping the snowbank took far more digging, pulling, and strategizing than he'd expected, but then he'd never had to tow a vehicle from a ditch filled with three feet of snow before.

He rolled up his window as he dictated a text to Adeline. "We lost half an hour to a ditch detour. ETA one hour."

He glanced at Tim, and the manager nodded, silently assuring him they could keep that time frame. Gannon sent the text, put the vehicle in gear, and retook the lead with a wave to the guys as he passed them. He didn't see Philip's response, but John saluted him.

"And people say I'm a bad winter driver," Tim grumbled.

Still flying on the high of getting out of the ditch, Gannon smiled instead of taking offense. "No, at this point, all they're saying about you is that you're no help."

As the other guys had helped shovel and tow, Tim remained in his seat, so caught up in his phone, it was a wonder the device hadn't combusted under his laser focus. "I'm the one making sure you don't get stuck twenty minutes from the cabin after all this."

"So what's the plan?" Because last he'd heard, nothing was plowed after the next turn.

Tim had said he'd made arrangements without sharing details. "In about ten minutes, we have to pull over and call in to a radio station."

Another stop? The last thing he wanted to do was chat with a DJ right now. "How'll that help?"

"The person who's agreed to help us requested a song. You're going to sing it live."

Gannon made a face. He had a guitar in back, but through the phone and radio, the sound quality would be awful. "What song?"

"'Not Your Hero.'"

The song he'd written after severing an unhealthy friendship with a needy actress last year had done pretty well for Awestruck. They'd performed it night after night on tour this year, but the lyrics didn't convey the warm message of reconciliation and love that went with the season. "Who would request that song on Christmas Eve?"

"His name is Clark."

"And he is ...?"

"Going through a divorce. That's all I'll tell you."

At least Gannon knew the lyrics. If this Clark guy had gone back a few albums, Gannon might've had to take extra time to study before singing, since he wouldn't go down as the guy who'd forgotten his own song on live radio. "They're not expecting the full band, right? Even if we found something for John to hit, there'd be no way to balance the sound."

"Just you, rock star. Eight minutes."

Hopefully they didn't lose any fans over this. "You warned the others?"

"Doing that now."

"Send Adeline the station info so she can listen if she wants. And tell the station I'm going to do a Christmas song too." It'd be quite the juxtaposition, going from the anger of "Not Your Hero" to a carol, but it was Christmas—almost, anyway—and though he hadn't known what to buy her, he did remember Adeline's favorite Christmas song.

Besides, if he had access to listeners today, he wouldn't go without celebrating the best gift he'd ever received.

$\sim$

ADELINE FIDDLED with the radio dial as Tegan pulled her feet up to sit cross-legged on the driver's seat of the Jeep.

"We could've used our phones inside."

"I didn't want to risk missing it." Adeline hit the seek button a couple of more times and landed on the station. She'd never listened to the radio over the internet, and it might've taken extra searching to find the right one. Tim had only given them two minutes of warning, so they'd yanked on coats and run in their socks to the garage.

Tegan had turned the key far enough to power the radio, leaving the engine off so they didn't have to open the garage door to the still-falling snow.

A song by a pop star named Michaela wound down. Missing Gannon over the last year, Adeline had watched all the seasons of the reality show he'd been a judge for, *Audition Room*, including the year he'd coached this singer to the win.

The DJ came on, introducing himself and the station. After some preamble, he welcomed Gannon and questioned him on the situation that had led to him calling in to perform a song.

The phone distorted some of the richness of Gannon's voice, but she could still listen to him talk all day. The quiet strains of him tuning his guitar floated in the background. Adeline drew her own feet up onto her seat and hugged her knees.

Gannon wrapped up his explanation. "Long story short, there's someone I'd really like to see today—the sooner, the better. My manager tells me this will help."

"Did he say how?"

"He did not, but he's served us well this far, and I'm happy to spread a little Christmas cheer."

"The song you're singing isn't very Christmassy." The DJ's grin came through loud and clear.

"That's true." Gannon picked at the strings as he spoke. "But after the request, I'm going to hang around to sing a carol, if that's all right with you."

"You can sing as many songs as you want."

"Here we go then. This one's for Clark." Gannon launched into "Not Your Hero."

Some of Awestruck's mellower songs landed on top hit playlists and enjoyed airtime on a variety of pop and rock stations, but this song was normally relegated to hard rock stations. Without Philip and John, the song sounded incomplete to Adeline, but hopefully Clark, whoever he was, enjoyed it.

When Gannon finished, the DJ cut in again.

Adeline strained to pick out the notes Gannon quietly picked while humoring the guy with small talk. Finally, the DJ invited him to take over for the second song.

"This one has a dual purpose." Gannon's voice became clearer, as if he'd moved the phone to a better spot. "I believe the message of the lyrics, but it also happens to be my girlfriend's favorite Christmas song."

How did he know her favorite Christmas song? Adeline wasn't even sure she knew.

Within a couple of chords, she recognized the hymn, and a slow smile built as the lyrics came back to her and, finally, the memory. They'd sung "O Holy Night" together as part of the congregation at a church service last year. She'd commented on how much she loved the song, and he must've remembered.

A garage didn't seem like a holy enough place to hear such a powerful voice sing such a perfect song. As the verse built and Gannon unleashed into the chorus, her throat ached to sing along, but she resisted. She was a musician in her own right, but she'd never had voice training, and she could add nothing to improve the sound of Gannon's performance.

At the last, "Christ is the Lord!" she caught a tear. Music was moving, was part of who she was and what had brought her and Gannon together, but it rarely drew a tear.

This time, though ... The emotion resulted from so many things. The man she loved sang the carol partly for her. Despite their misunderstandings and disappointments, he'd remembered her favorite song. He loved God enough to make worship a priority, even when he'd called in to a secular radio station. And, the song itself was powerful worship of a God who'd loved her enough to come into her broken world and suffer in order to save her.

The final chords faded, and she blinked open her eyes.

Next to her, Tegan leaned her head against the window, listening intently.

The DJ also seemed touched, but his awe only lasted a sentence or two before he started chatting about lighter subjects. A minute later, they wound down by trading wishes for merry Christmases.

When Gannon disconnected, she and Tegan returned to the living area of the cabin. All three dogs awaited them, making progress to the kitchen difficult. Finally, Adeline reached the freezer, which brimmed with pre-made meals.

"The guys should be here in time for lunch. Chicken pot pie?" One of her own favorite comfort foods.

Tegan nodded. "But what do you think that Clark guy is going to do to help them?"

"I guess we'll have to wait and see."

ohn hated what he had to do, so he'd put it off.

First, he'd figured he ought to let the truth sink in, let his frustration and anger cool.

They'd listened to the radio. Maintaining silence was even easier when Gannon wiped out into the ditch, since John helped tow him out. Talking over "O Holy Night" would've been sacrilege, though John hadn't been able to resist drumming on the steering wheel for "Not Your Hero."

Afterward, when they'd resumed their course down the road, Nicole had shut off the stereo.

The silence had been heavy with impending doom.

In truth, he waited, not because he needed more time or he doubted his conclusions but because he—wow, this was hard to admit, even to himself—he didn't want to end up alone.

He preferred enduring quiet suspicion to dodging pity from Gannon and Adeline at the cabin. To touring a house knowing he had no prospects for a family to fill it. To showing up solo to his family's Christmas, where each of his sisters would be with their significant others.

They reached the last country highway. Every other road up

to that point had been plowed at least once, reducing the accumulation. Not the last road, though. Fourteen inches of snow blanketed the asphalt between them and their destination, and any dip or rise in the road would mean drifts even the Jacked and Twisted vehicles couldn't overcome.

Instead of making the turn, Gannon pulled as far to the side of the road as he could without getting stuck again, and the others followed suit.

Tim says his solution is coming, Gannon's text read.

John studied the only structure in sight, a long-abandoned gas station, out his driver's side window.

Twenty minutes later, the wait continued, and the atmosphere had grown as intolerable as the air in a parked car on a one-hundred-degree day.

"Doesn't that hurt your fingers?" Nicole asked.

John shook his head and kept drumming the beat to "Not Your Hero." The lyrics fit the direction his day was going. To think, twenty-four hours ago, he'd been oblivious. Nic's cards still hadn't declined. She hadn't turned up her nose at his gift. He hadn't heard about the skipped gigs.

What a difference a day made.

What would change by tomorrow? Would he be able to breathe again?

Only if he surrendered his commitment to silence. He stared at the black opening in the gas station, a broken window. "Tell me about these missed gigs."

"Missed gigs?"

He stopped drumming, turned toward her, and studied those lioness eyes. "Renee talked with me last night."

"Why?" Her bewilderment seemed genuine.

The rep from the agency must not have mentioned their conversation. That explained why Nicole hadn't raised the subject—she hadn't realized Renee had tipped him off. But that didn't mean he could back off.

"She says you're unreliable. She wanted me to talk you into showing up for work."

She shifted in her seat, emotions flashing across her face. Offense. Dismay. Maybe embarrassment.

Outside, the wind launched eddies of snow.

"I had a chance to go to Rio. What was I supposed to do? Pass that up?"

"If you had a commitment ..." He lifted his hand. The only time he'd missed a show was due to appendicitis. He'd hated knowing someone else was filling in for him with Awestruck. He never would've missed over a vacation. "It sounded like you missed more than one gig."

"I missed one for *Magnetism Magazine* too. You remember Richard?"

"Yes." He'd met the guy at one of Nicole's shows. The fashion designer had been a little too friendly with her for John's tastes.

"He's starting his own label, and he needed someone on short notice to show off his line for some investors, so of course he called me."

"And you went, despite a prior commitment."

"He's a dear friend, and because of me, he got the backing he needs."

John would rather be out of the vehicle, exploring the trees or the gas station in the wind and snow, than inside, exploring this subject. But what choice did he have? "Were those the only two you missed?"

"What are you? My father?"

Frustration rose, but he refused to let his volume go along for the ride. "What's going on, Nicole?"

"I didn't know I had to run my schedule by you."

Fair enough. But she'd fallen through on commitments— probably more than twice, given the way she'd cut off the line of questioning. "If your cards declined because of money trouble, missing gigs would only make matters worse."

She shook her head, looked at the ceiling of the truck, and shook her head again. The extra sheen in her eyes caught flecks of light. "You're judging me?"

"I'm asking for the truth."

"So debt is a deal breaker for you."

"Lying is a deal breaker."

She swiped at one of her eyes, removing tears. "I thought you were serious about us. When you said you wanted to spend Christmas together and you wanted me to meet your family ..." She left the blank for him to fill.

What was she getting at?

"Life is expensive." Her voice lowered, and the skin above her eyebrows bunched. "It's not like you couldn't get me out of debt in an instant if you wanted to, and is that really so much to ask? Aren't I worth it?"

He clenched his jaw as he clicked through her statements, added them up. "You thought I'd pay your way while you blew off work, maxed out your cards, and lied to me?"

"I thought you loved me."

His disbelief caught in his throat. He wanted their relationship to progress. He wanted to love her, but with the tour this year, there'd been too much time apart, too much distance.

And, apparently, too many lies.

"To be clear, you've been massively in debt this whole time."

"You're painting me like a terrible person."

"Nic." He'd thought her too smart to defend blatant dishonesty.

"You make millions every year."

So did she. She could've lived within her means. She hadn't, and worse, she'd lied to hide it. Had possibly been more interested in his money than him this whole time.

He should've confronted all this back in Chicago, where a breakup would've been easier.

Yet he'd already chosen denial far too long. "We have nothing without honesty."

Her chin lifted, fire in her eyes. "Fine. Get out, then."

"And you'll what?"

"Drive myself back to Chicago."

John unbuckled, angry enough to let her. At least this would be a clean break. A miserable drive back for her, but she'd asked for it. Out of habit, he reached for the keys, then paused. He would have to entrust the vehicle to her. "You'll get this back to Jacked and Twisted?"

"You think that little of me?"

He narrowly resisted nodding. "Do you need money for gas?"

Nicole let out a hissing sigh. "I have some cash. I don't want your money."

A rueful laugh darted past his commitment to being the better person. If she didn't want his money, she ought to fling that bracelet at him.

He'd already given her enough, so he took her at her word. Later, he could follow up with the shop, make sure they got the truck back or were compensated for it. He grabbed the coat she didn't want from the back seat, hit the button to open the tailgate, and circled to the back of the vehicle. Snow pinged against his neck as he collected his overnight bag and the shopping bags that contained his gifts for his family. Loaded down with all his belongings, he started toward Gannon's SUV.

The driver door of the truck he'd shared with Nicole popped open directly in front of him, narrowly missing his face. She dropped in front of him. "You want to talk about honesty?"

He waited for the accusation. Whatever it was, he'd fire it down. He'd been nothing but honest with her.

"You wouldn't tell me what happened with your biological dad."

She couldn't have surprised him more if she'd launched a snowball at his face.

"And?"

"That proves there are things you wouldn't tell me either."

It proved he'd known on some level all along he couldn't trust her. Why would he share his most personal story? "I didn't lie."

"Didn't have to." A scornful scowl marred her features. Even she couldn't pull off a look that ugly. "I could tell what kind of relationship you wanted, and it wasn't the no-holds-barred, honest kind."

He ground his teeth. If he had to explain the difference between his secrets and hers, the endeavor wasn't worth the breath. He tightened his hold on the bags and shifted to step around her.

"You're going to regret walking away. You would've gotten at least as much out of this relationship as I did. Men would kill to be with me."

"Then find one of them to con." He stepped around her and drew the cold winter air into his lungs.

～

TIM SWORE UNDER HIS BREATH. "He's coming. What are we supposed to say?"

"Knowing John? Nothing." Words already jammed up in Gannon's throat, but the last thing John would want were questions or platitudes.

As someone who valued his privacy, John would probably prefer no one had witnessed the argument.

Gannon and Tim's spectatorship had been accidental. Tim said whatever arrangement he'd made would arrive any

79

moment, so Gannon watched the road and checked the mirrors to see if anything was approaching from behind. That's how he'd spotted John getting out of his truck, a white coat in hand.

Odd.

When John came back into view with his luggage and shopping bags, Gannon realized what must've happened. Nicole hopped out to confront him. John said about two words before stepping around her and continuing toward Gannon and Tim's vehicle.

A message with a lone question mark arrived from Philip.

I think that was a breakup, Gannon texted back.

John rapped on the rear window, and Gannon unlocked the tailgate. John grunted his frustration—the back was full—and came around to the side door. He plunked his bags in the seat next to him and buckled in.

The rumble of a large vehicle sounded on the road. Nicole had already pulled a U-turn and driven off. Now, an orange county plow advanced down the street. When the vehicle stopped next to Gannon's window, the massive curved blade stood at least three times as high as the smaller ones used farther south in the state.

Tim hopped out.

Gannon reached for his own door handle but glanced at John.

Anger hardened the drummer's expression, and he focused out the window, on the plow.

Gannon ought to say something. John never failed to tell him exactly what he needed to hear—even when Gannon wasn't a willing audience. There must be something Gannon could say to make this just a fraction easier.

"You did the right thing."

John dipped his chin.

Outside, Tim met the middle-aged plow operator with a handshake, and both looked toward the driver seat of the SUV.

Gannon was required for one more meet and greet, apparently, and because he wasn't doing any good with John, he got out.

Clark, the driver, immediately apologized to Gannon for being late.

"No problem," Tim said. "To make it up to us, you could take a pass up the private drive to the cabin itself."

Clark nodded twice, looked to Gannon, and nodded again. "Sure."

"I don't want you to pay for our Christmas plans with your job." Gannon shoved his cold hands deep in his pockets. "The county's okay with this?"

"We're covering the extra fuel and overtime," Tim said. "It's all approved."

"We're all out anyway, and this road needed to be cleared, so you're doing the county a favor." Clark pulled off his hat, smacked it against the thigh of his jeans, and tugged it back over his gray-smattered hair. "Thanks for the song. It was shaping up to be a pretty awful Christmas, but this'll be a story for the grandkids."

Tim waved to the SUVs, and Philip and John joined them. A few pictures later, they returned to their trucks.

Tim guffawed when the plow cut through a mound of snow similar to the one that had landed Gannon in the ditch. The blades sent the accumulation rolling toward the shoulders, leaving behind the clearest path they'd driven since Chicago.

"We'll be there in no time," Tim promised.

Gannon nodded, but a *thunk* reverberated against his seat. John had been all smiles outside, but now he'd leaned forward, out of view of the mirror. Presumably, it was his head he'd smacked against the seat.

Gannon put the SUV in drive and pulled forward. "Hang in there, buddy."

"Yup."

Tim glanced back, then shot Gannon a concerned look.

Not much they could do about it.

Gannon followed the plow at enough of a distance that the salt shedding from the dispenser in back wouldn't pour straight into the grill of the SUV. Besides, he needed enough reaction time to stop slowly if needed because John's head continued pressing against the back of his seat. A sudden stop could cause an injury.

He'd ended up with precious cargo after all.

9

*B*eing fired from Awestruck hadn't changed Matt, but finding August Peltier dead had.

Parked in front of his parent's home, Matt wasn't so sure he could maintain those changes.

He could really use a line right now.

A hit. A drink.

Anything to take the edge off seeing the collective judgment, pity, and disappointment on his family's faces when he walked up to the door.

He'd spent years so bent on staying high and drunk that he hadn't even missed Awestruck when Gannon cut him loose. He'd reveled in the freedom and found a new band that would revel with him. He and August, the lead singer, sought out highs wherever they could be found.

But then Matt found Augie dead.

Dead, Augie hadn't been able to pass him his next high, crack some inappropriate joke, or even blink. For once, Augie couldn't hide anything from Matt. Literally. His eyes had been open, and he'd been naked.

Matt pulled a sheet over him and called the police. He'd

waited outside, trying to clear the image from his mind, but he couldn't then. He couldn't now.

In a dream, instead of Augie on the floor, Matt saw himself lying there.

When he woke, he hadn't been able to name a single person who'd care enough to pull a sheet over him. Everyone who cared—Gannon and John included—had left or sent him away.

He'd checked himself into rehab the day of Augie's funeral. He'd been off drugs and alcohol—and women—ever since.

But the prospect of facing his family without the numbing of alcohol or drugs and without the distractions of fame and women left his palms sweaty and his heart pounding. He'd been a daredevil back in the day, drawn to action sports and jumping out of airplanes. He'd taken countless risks as an addict.

None scared him as badly as risking his family's rejection by showing up here for Christmas. Sure, Mom would be glad to see him. Krissy might too. But Pete wouldn't be, and though he'd hurt Mom these last few years, he'd spent a lifetime disappointing Dad.

It'd started with unimpressive grades, a disinterest in traditional sports, and a little too much interest in girls and BMX. And then moving to California with a band—a plan his dad literally laughed at. Finally, Matt seemed to have vindicated himself when Awestruck succeeded, but that flashed and burned out faster than a faulty light bulb.

Four months clean wasn't enough to erase a lifetime of failure. Not when he'd tried and failed the whole rehab thing a couple of years before. Dad would require some serious proof before forgiving and accepting him again.

It was only fair. Matt had fallen short on every front and hurt everyone who'd ever cared about him. He'd turned his back on his faith. He'd barely managed to hang onto a terrible apartment, and given the state of his finances, even that might not last long.

He had no excuse for himself.

No way to help himself.

No one to blame but himself.

And very little progress to point to, considering he was sitting in his car and longing for a substance to abuse on Christmas Eve.

Christmas.

Two thousand years ago, a nativity scene played out. He believed that. He believed all the stuff he'd heard about Jesus except one thing—grace. Free grace.

Matt didn't deserve a free pass. Well, no. Not free. Paid for by Jesus on the cross. If access to heaven were a free ticket, like backstage passes fans won sometimes, he might justify taking it. But one as costly as salvation, paid for by someone else?

It was too much.

He got out of his car. He deserved to have nothing to dull his emotions. A man like him deserved all the judgment his family could muster.

It'd snowed hard overnight, but now, only light flurries descended, gentle and too sparse to fill the footprints of the others who had arrived before him. A shovel leaned against the siding by the entry. Matt grabbed the tool and took it to the sidewalk, clearing every inch. When he finished that, he shoved it back and forth up the driveway, hefting off the eight or ten inches the area had gotten.

He leveled the shovel against the walk between the door and drive. A few more swipes, and it'd be time to face the music. He took one trip toward the door and doubled back, clearing the other half of the walk.

"Matt?"

He froze, but he wasn't used to the labor of shoveling. His ravenous need to inhale forced his lungs back into motion. He tried to control his panting as he turned. His mom and sister stood in the doorway, faces splashed with surprise.

He had accepted Mom's invitation, but after all the times he'd let them down, he couldn't hold a little shock against them.

Man. Those two looked too ... sweet. Innocent. Homey. Bright. Naive. He couldn't find the right word, but whatever the word should be, it was the opposite of Matt. They were clean. Through and through. They'd never used drugs, other than those legally prescribed, but this was more than that. He had a whole slew of experiences on them, ugly experiences. The kinds that were anything but clean.

They'd never found a dead body, for one.

Krissy wore a fuzzy Santa hat. Mom, an apron. His older brother would be inside somewhere, doing something responsible like helping Mom in the kitchen or assisting Dad with—

"Who's here?" Dad stepped up behind the other two, hands lifted as if he meant to put one on the shoulder of each. He stilled, however, when his gaze landed on Matt.

Matt had called Mom from rehab, but his father wouldn't be impressed until he'd proven himself, something he still didn't know how to do. He'd hoped to get inside before the man saw him so they could stay on opposite sides of the room and ignore each other.

Dad edged his hands between Mom and Krissy, parting them. He stepped onto the stoop, and Matt looked away. But hurried footsteps on the walk drew his attention back. Dad pulled him to his chest in a giant hug.

Matt's head spun. A punch, he would've understood, but this? He didn't lift his own arms to return the hug because, any moment, Dad would come to his senses, remember who Matt was, what he'd done. How very likely he was to do it again.

Dad settled his hands on Matt's shoulders. "Why are you shoveling?"

The question came so out of left field, he couldn't conjure an answer.

Dad pulled the handle from his cold fingers, stuck the tool in the snow, and put an arm around his shoulders to lead him into the house.

"We're glad you're here," Mom said.

He believed her, but he studied his old man's face for signs this was an act he'd give up as soon as Mom returned to the kitchen.

He found none.

He opened his mouth to apologize, but would Dad understand for how much?

At the door, Dad patted his back to send him in.

Matt scratched his forehead.

Pete lurked inside, forehead drawn in the expression Matt had expected from everyone. But Krissy smiled and hugged him. Mom laughed and said something about her prodigal with such joy that he couldn't take offense. Anyway, he knew the story of the prodigal son, the one who returned home after he found himself longing to steal food from a pig. That guy understood low points and how out of place Matt felt here.

Dad shut the door, closing him into their home.

A four-year-old girl scampered up behind Krissy, curious but hiding. His niece, Jade. He hadn't seen her since she was a baby.

Krissy lay a hand on her head. "Say hi to your Uncle Matt."

She tilted shining eyes up toward him, but instead of saying hi, she shouted, "Merry Christmas!"

~

ADELINE TURNED the oven as low as it would go. The pot pie had finished cooking, but something had delayed the guys. She checked her phone for the tenth time. Still nothing. "They would've told us if they'd gotten moving again, right? If Tim's help came?"

Tegan gave a sympathetic smile. "Maybe we should eat. They can always reheat what they want when they get here."

When they get here. That should've been twenty minutes ago. Their arrival seemed both imminent and impossible.

A sound like thunder crashed in the woods and rolled closer. "A plow?"

Tegan joined her in hurrying to the window. Sure enough, a big plow swept before the cabin and followed the loop around. It stopped on the far side, aimed to go back down the lane, but at the moment, it couldn't, because a pair of big trucks—SUVs, technically—rolled down the drive.

Finally!

As quickly as Adeline rushed for the entry, John's dogs beat her to it. By the time she got the door open, Bruce had joined the group. They all spilled across the generous porch, down the steps, and over the snow the plow left piled at the side of the drive.

Gannon exited the far side of the front vehicle and jogged to meet her, catching her up in his arms, solid and strong. When he let her down again, he threaded his fingers into her hair and kissed her as if they weren't in the middle of a crowd. Kissed her as if he'd been waiting for this with even more anticipation than she had.

His lips were a warm contrast to the air chilling her face, and his body heat radiated through her sweater. Their separations were, at times, almost unbearable. Impossible miles, sharing him with the whole wide world, always having a time set when they'd have to say goodbye again. The ache of separation had flavored her year.

But there was nothing quite like a reunion kiss.

A whoop sounded from somewhere in the peanut gallery.

Gannon's hazel eyes opened as he lifted his lips from hers.

He seemed slow to focus, like he'd woken from a dream, but his attention remained on her.

Adeline slid her hands across his T-shirt and around his waist, under his unzipped coat. Her inhale brought the scent of sandalwood mixed with the wintery woods that surrounded them.

A second whoop sounded.

Tim had opened his door, but the noise came from farther off.

"Is that the plow driver?" she asked.

The corner of his mouth edged up. "His name is Clark. We're restoring his faith in love." He bent to kiss her again.

She let him, but only for a moment. He might not mind an audience, but she did. She stepped back, snow packing against the knit of her socks. Tim took note, shook his head, and wandered toward the back of the SUV, mumbling about crazy people.

The plow honked. Gannon waved, as did Philip, who'd climbed out of the second SUV. Clark rumbled back down the lane.

Adeline refocused on those getting out of the vehicles. She'd already spotted Tim and Philip, and now Philip's parents. Presumably, they'd get the kids out next. But Gannon had sent a picture of three vehicles. "No John and Nicole?"

"No Nicole." Gannon glanced around and lowered his voice. "She's headed back to Chicago. She's been lying about money."

Adeline cringed. "How is he?"

Gannon tilted his head. "Haven't had the chance to corner him into talking yet."

Never an easy task with John. Where was he, anyway?

"Where are your shoes?" A girl in a yellow coat stood about eight feet away. Her light brown, shoulder-length hair struggled to escape a barrette that must've been in all night.

Gannon finally looked down at Adeline's feet and laughed.

"Aren't you cold?" the girl asked.

She hesitated to answer. Gannon kept her from noticing the cold seeping through her socks, but she probably shouldn't encourage Philip's daughter to run outside so carelessly.

Gannon must've taken her hesitation for an answer to the affirmative, because in one swift move, he'd swept her off her feet. She squealed and fastened her arms around him when he half-climbed, half-slid through the deep, dense snow left by the plow. He carried her up the steps and set her on the porch, where the overhang blocked the snow.

"Carry me, Dad!" Nila hopped in front of Philip, despite his full load of luggage.

"And me!" Philip's younger child, Nason, tore around the SUV to grab Philip's hand.

Philip let the luggage fall and picked the kids up with a roar that ignited their giggles. He spun them in a couple of circles, their boots skimming the snow, before depositing them on the steps and going back for the bags.

John stepped from behind the SUV Gannon had driven, the straps of a black bag slung over one shoulder. His dogs trotted after him, tongues lolling and tails whipping. While the others treated the snow pile like a piece of playground equipment, John marched over it like a defeated soldier.

Even his smile of greeting looked weary.

When he got close enough, she hugged him, a little tighter than normal.

He gave her another heart-wrenching smile for the effort. "Thanks for taking care of my dogs."

"Of course. Anything you need. Ever."

He seemed to almost laugh at that, but instead of replying, he motioned for her to head inside.

10

The low strains of an upright bass reverberated from the library. Philip looked in as he passed. Large swaths of gift wrap lay on the floor, discarded, as Adeline drew her bow across the strings. In addition to the upright double bass she played, two others stood by the wall. Gannon looked as if he would drift off on the couch as he listened, but absorbed in playing, Adeline didn't seem to mind.

Philip wouldn't argue with a nap himself, but Nila and Nason had graduated from them and were raring to go. With Dad and Joan asleep, entertaining his kids fell to him. He found them watching John suit up his dogs for a walk.

"Dogs wear boots?" Nila once again gripped her locket, rubbing her thumb over the surface, though her attention was riveted on Trigger.

"Salt hurts their feet."

"But that's snow outside."

"It's on the road." John caught another of the gray dog's paws and slipped a boot on it. Finished, he let the dog go.

The kids sounded peals of laughter as Trigger high-stepped,

uncomfortable with the gear. Even John smiled as he prepped Camo.

"You two get your boots and coats on too," Philip said. "We'll see if we can make a fort."

Cheering, the kids disappeared into the closet where they'd hung the coats and stashed their boots. John and his dogs made it out the door before the kids finished suiting up. When they stepped outside, the drummer was already out of sight.

The clouds were dissipating, and in the sun, the snow would pack best, so Philip steered his kids toward the patch of light in the center of the looped drive.

He'd expected them to get bored and cold, but their attention spans surprised him. They barely noticed when John brought the dogs back and left again in one of the trucks, headed off to see a property.

Long after that, the kids were still happy when Dad came out and sat on the porch steps. Philip had helped create and push six large disks of snow into place, forming three-foot-tall walls. Nason busily packed snow into the spaces between the disks, while Nila worked to clear a doorway. Both of them remained so absorbed in their work, they didn't complain when he left to sit next to his dad.

The evergreen garland tied to the railings added extra pine scent to the forest air. "I didn't think they'd be so well rested after a night in the van," Philip said.

"One of the many benefits of youth. But you'll want to start bedtime routines right after dinner. They'll head downhill fast."

Right. Bedtime routines were his responsibility, no one else's. He pulled off his gloves to rub his numb hands together. "Joan asked me what I'm going to do the next time we go on tour."

"Ah." Dad's shoulders rose and fell with a long breath. "We're getting older, Philip, and so are they. One year here, one year there ..." Dad lifted his hands and turned a steady gaze on him. "It's a lot for them. They need the stability of a life in one place, and we're thrilled to be grandparents, but we can't be parents again. We're past that stage of life."

Philip put his gloves back on and interlaced his fingers. "What if I passed it, too, when Clare died? What if I never ... had it?"

Nason threw a snowball over the wall, and Nila squealed and ran. By the time she circled back, she carried three of her own snowballs to launch inside the fort.

"You're not just worried about travel," Dad said.

Philip rubbed his hand over his mouth. "It was supposed to be that I would provide for Clare, and she would make sure they had a nice home and the care they needed. The school supplies, the clothes, the haircuts ... The little barrettes."

Dad chuckled. "Those are one hundred percent Joan."

"They were supposed to be one hundred percent Clare."

Nason wailed inside the fort. One of the snowballs Nila lobbed over must've hit its target. Philip trudged through the snow and lifted his son over the fort wall. He checked him over, calmed him down, and brought the children in.

He and his dad found a hot chocolate mix with tiny marsh-mallows.

"You sure you don't want one?" Dad stirred cocoa into a third mug.

"I'm good." Philip passed cups to the kids.

They set the children up at the dining table with the hot chocolate and some activity books, and his dad motioned him to accompany him to the living room. Someone suggested they hold a Christmas Eve service this evening, but for now, everyone still seemed to be off doing their own thing.

Dad slurped from his mug before setting it on the coffee table. He glanced at the tree that dominated the recessed area by the bay windows, but the decorations and cocoa wouldn't keep him distracted long. Philip felt like a guilty man awaiting a judge's sentence.

"I can't imagine what it'd be like to spend a year off touring the world and come back and crash land into family life. But you've done this before, and you'll figure it out again. You're the very best thing for your kids, and they're the best thing for you."

He'd thought that about Clare, but God must not've agreed. "I love them. I just don't know how to be everything for them. It feels impossible."

Dad nodded. "What's even more unlikely than you finding a way is Clare coming back."

Heat washed over him. Dad really thought that needed to be said?

"You've patched together one temporary solution after another since she died, son." Dad winced, as if the words hurt to say. "It's time to accept that this is how life is and enact a permanent solution. Joan and I can't be that. It's not fair to anyone. The good news is, you don't have to be everything to them. You just have to be their father."

"And their mother, if Clare's not coming back." Which she wasn't. Why had he said "if"? Maybe Dad was right. He'd never come to terms with that, with the need to find a permanent solution.

"You're a single parent," Dad said, "and that's a big responsibility, but unless God provides someone to step in where Clare left off, your kids have a dad, not a mom. It's less than ideal, but it's also doable, especially if you're making wise choices, the kinds that keep the kids' best interests at heart." He gave a loaded glance.

A blade of meaning pierced Philip's chest. Trying to cope after Clare's death, he'd made some poor choices. Relied on things he shouldn't have. More temporary solutions. But joining Awestruck meant signing a morality agreement, so now he had one more reason not to go back to old habits. He wanted to provide for his kids, and Awestruck was key to that. He wouldn't gamble with his kids or his job.

He just wished no one knew how he'd failed, wished Dad would quit alluding to it. Wished those old habits didn't occur to him when he wondered how to cope after the tour.

His father laid a hand on his shoulder. "You don't have to be everything. Just Dad. You can do that."

Philip nodded. *Just Dad.*

Because Clare was gone.

~

WHEN JOHN STARTED the drive up to the Lakeshore area, he'd planned to send word to his family that he'd broken up with Nicole. He didn't want to deal with their surprise and questions in person. But sending the message would make the end official, so he'd let navigating the snowy roads distract him.

He'd seen a few plows since leaving the cabin, and most roads had been at least partially cleared, but at a few junctions, he'd been grateful for the SUV's capabilities. He owned a four-wheel-drive sedan, but living in this remote area might require him to get something lifted.

Or a snowmobile? In this area, residents relied heavily on them.

He slowed for what GPS said would be the last turn before the driveway. The little road tunneled through the snowy woods.

The countryside place was restful. Peaceful.

Even if he had no one to someday share it with.

He sighed.

A black-and-red for-sale sign hung on a rusted old gate that flanked an even narrower drive. Looked like someone had scraped most of the snow from the driveway with a pickup plow, leaving a flat, packed layer behind. He followed the drive and soon came to a wider cleared area.

Ahead stood the house, but not the traditional front view. Instead, the garage made up the face of the building, and from the looks of the trees, no road circled past the front door. The owners must always come and go through the garage doors or the small utility door to the side of them. From the online pictures, however, he knew there was a nice exterior door somewhere.

He pulled up next to the late-model sedan parked by one of the garage doors. Nicole would hate this place. Not showy enough for her, but he liked that the house didn't lead with its most charming features.

Easier to trust that way.

Besides, he was glad he had never fully opened up to Nicole. Had been a little hard to get to know.

Kind of like this house was to first-time visitors.

He rubbed his face. If he was identifying with a building, the events of the last day were getting to him.

Even so, he'd known from the very start that Awestruck couldn't complete him or be his life's sole purpose. Hence the pains he took to keep his role as Awestruck's drummer separate from his core identity. The bracelets he put on and took off served as a small reminder of a larger, vital truth.

And then Nicole had gone and used him—who he was away from the crowd—to capitalize on what he could offer as Awestruck's drummer.

If Nicole, famous herself, had set her sights on his bank accounts, who was above suspicion? Because of her, he'd wonder about motives every time he met someone—unless that someone somehow didn't know about Awestruck.

He stretched both hands up and settled them behind his headrest.

His time with Nicole had needed to end.

And he couldn't put off telling his family forever.

He typed out the message. *Nicole and I have gone our separate ways. She won't be with me tomorrow.*

Hank, his stepdad, would probably take that at face value, but his mom and sisters would reply with questions he didn't want to deal with. He silenced his phone as he got out of the car.

A shoveled path led around the side of the home. By following that, he found the real estate agent taking one last swipe of snow off the stoop of the main entrance.

Inside, he stowed his shoes on the utility mat, and the old hardwood creaked a welcome beneath his feet. The baseboards and door trim gleamed, though the finish had texture that came only with age. The place was dim and worn, but tidy, as the pictures online had led him to expect.

He and the real estate agent talked about adding windows, skylights, and a deck, about keeping a staircase the previous owner had handcrafted, preserving most of the old woodwork, and updating the kitchen.

By the time he left, he wanted the place, but he stopped himself from signing any paperwork. If he wasn't in the right mindset to read texts from his family, he had no business buying a house.

~

"THAT'S NOT A BASS." Nila scrunched her nose.

Once Adeline unwrapped the basses from Gannon after lunch, they'd talked. Then, his need to sleep and her desire to try the instruments dovetailed nicely. She'd spent most of the afternoon playing while he drifted in and out, sometimes sleeping, sometimes talking about the instruments or a piece she'd played.

About twenty minutes ago, he'd excused himself to take a

shower before dinner. Adeline had been about to pack up the bass and go help with the meal when Nila appeared in the doorway.

"It is a bass." Holding the neck, Adeline stepped aside so Nila could get a good look. "But it's called an upright double bass. Your dad plays a different kind—an electric bass."

"Oh." Nila chewed her lip. "Do you know any songs?"

"Do you want me to play you one?" She could probably piece together "Jesus Loves Me" from memory.

Nila knelt and petted Bruce's graying head, her lips pressed together in thought. "Can you play 'Amazing Grace'?"

Wow. Philip's daughter had sophisticated taste for a kid. Adeline played the hymn often enough at church, but her part didn't include the melody, which Nila would most likely expect to hear. She used her phone to pull up the notes and drew her bow across the strings.

A few beats in, Nila's sweet voice rose to accompany the low sound of the instrument.

The little girl knew every word of the first verse and most of the others.

When they finished, Adeline clapped for her. "How do you know that song?"

Bruce had returned to his napping, but Nila continued to focus on him as she stroked his thick fur. "My mom used to sing it to me."

The poor, sweet child.

Adeline missed Gannon when he traveled, but Nila's mom wasn't coming home. She longed to wrap her in a hug, but she might do best to work with the connection they'd found in music.

She set her bow aside. "Would you like to play too? I can hold the strings, so all you have to do is pluck the note. We'll do it together."

Nila straightened away from the dog. "We can play Mom's song?"

"It would be an honor."

They spent the next ten minutes learning to play the first line together. They'd completed a pretty good run when a quiet sound drew her attention to the door. Philip stood in the entry, eyes on his daughter. Adeline hadn't gotten to know him very well over the last year, but that looked like pain in his expression.

The section complete, Nila gave her a gap-toothed smile. "I did it!"

"You did. Great job." Adeline lent enthusiasm to her voice and gave the girl a high five because she didn't deserve to have her excitement squashed, even if Adeline never should've agreed to work on a song with her that might resurrect painful memories for Philip. "Looks like your dad missed you. You'd better go with him now."

As Nila turned toward her father, Adeline watched him force a smile. He too congratulated the girl on a job well done.

"Can we sing that tonight?" Nila asked. "Like we used to?"

"Of course." Philip smoothed his hand over her curls as she cheered at his response and slipped past him into the hall. Before stepping away himself, he lifted his focus to Adeline, his smile growing less and less convincing, what with the wound in his eyes. "Thank you."

"No. I'm sorry. She said her mom used to sing it. I didn't mean to dredge anything up."

Philip nodded, chest expanding with a deep breath. "It's good. I don't think she really remembers her mom, but she knows that song." He shoved his fingers into his pockets. "It's brought a lot of comfort to her over the years. I want her to have that."

The set of his shoulders, the turn of his lips, the way he wouldn't hold eye contact more than a second all said he was hurting, and now it was Philip Adeline wanted to hug. That wasn't her place, but she would send Gannon after him later, even if it meant less time for her to spend with him.

That, after all, was an important part of Christmas. Sacrifice in the name of love.

11

*N*ason bounced on his bed as Philip came near to tuck him in.

"Did you brush your teeth?"

On an upward trajectory, the boy opened his mouth wide and breathed on Philip's face.

"Nice, buddy." Philip wiped off the drop of his son's spit that had landed on his lip and motioned him to lie down.

Nason kicked both legs out, flopped to the mattress, and squirmed under the covers. The second hot chocolate and the slice of cake for dessert had been mistakes. Too much sugar. Or was it just that tomorrow was Christmas?

Nila crouched by her suitcase on the far side of the other twin bed. He pulled down the covers for her. "Come on. Get in bed, and we'll sing the song."

She ignored him, pawing through her assortment of pink and purple clothing.

"Nila."

She turned teary eyes toward him.

Oh, not again.

"What's wrong, sweetheart?"

"Mom is gone."

At the teary declaration, he suddenly wasn't much more composed than his daughter.

Nila clutched a fist in front of her collarbone, where her locket had hung earlier.

"You mean the necklace?" he asked.

She nodded and turned back to her luggage.

Philip knelt beside her and helped her search. By the time they determined the locket wasn't among her clothes, her nose was dripping and Nason vaulted from one bed to the other. Philip handed her a tissue, asked both kids to climb in bed, and stole down the hall to check the bathroom.

No necklace.

He returned to tuck the kids in properly. Nason was still jumping.

"In bed. The sooner you sleep, the sooner tomorrow will be here, and you know what that means."

"Presents!" Nason plopped down.

Philip tucked him in, kissed his forehead, and turned to his still-crying daughter. Was he a monster for making her go to bed while the locket was still missing?

"I need my necklace."

He nodded, tucking the blankets around her. "I'll look for it."

Her voice rose an octave when she added, "I miss Mom."

He brushed her hair away from her face. "Me too. If I can't find the locket, I'll get you another one."

This brought a fresh welling of tears. "I don't want another one. I want *my* mom."

His heart cracked. He didn't want to replace Clare either. He wanted her back like he wanted air. He needed to get out of here before he blubbered like Nila. "We'll find the necklace. I promise."

She sniffled. "Will you sing the song?"

He'd hoped she'd forgotten because his voice might not hold. "Only one verse tonight so I can look for the necklace, okay?"

The poor kid agreed, so he sat on the edge of the twin bed and choked out the first verse of "Amazing Grace," his mind as far from the lyrics and memories as he could manage. When he finished, Nila's eyes remained red, but no new tears fell. He kissed her forehead, turned out the light, and left to try to keep his promise.

He found the dining table where they'd all eaten dinner together cleared, the dishes piled by the sink. They'd washed a few, but most waited for the maid who'd come in the morning —and would receive an exorbitant tip for working on Christmas, if Philip knew Gannon at all.

The decluttered surfaces made it easy to see the locket wasn't on the counters or the table. He moved aside the garland that still lay across the center and looked under the table and chairs.

No sign of it.

He followed the sound of Gannon's guitar to the living room. Everyone else had gathered for their service.

"Has anyone seen a heart locket?" If he could find it right away, he could get it to Nila before she fell asleep. Maybe she wouldn't have nightmares that way. Besides, finding it would mean one less piece of them was missing. Tiny as it was, that mattered. "It's Nila's. Has a picture of Clare in it."

Dad and Joan had sat at attention immediately, but now, with murmurs of concern, everyone rose and started checking the cracks between cushions, asking questions about where she'd been today and where he'd already checked.

One by one, they straightened, empty-handed.

"Outside?" John asked.

Philip groaned. They'd spent hours playing in the snow. If the chain broke, the locket could be mixed into fourteen inches of accumulation. "I hope not. I promised her I'd find it. I'll go check her room again and the hall. You guys don't have to wait for me."

But when he came back, he found half the group on hands and knees, searching the dining and living rooms. The others—Tim, Gannon, and John—were outside.

"You guys really don't have to do this."

Adeline poked her head up over the back of the couch. "Of course we do. If it's important to Nila, it's important to us. Awestruck's family. Just ask the guys."

The locket wasn't only important to Nila. She'd already been asleep when he'd gone back in the room and used his phone's light to scan the carpet, under the bed, in the corners, and on the dresser. Philip needed that necklace. Needed it for himself.

He pulled on his coat and boots and used his phone to scan the cracks in the porch. The boards fit close together, so the necklace shouldn't have been able to fall through. He moved on to check the stairs.

Tim worked closest to him, shining his own phone into the footprints pressed into the wall of snow left by the plow along the drive. "Probably shouldn't have made any promises about this one."

"I know." Philip ran his bare hands through the snow on either side of the steps. After the first couple of seconds, he couldn't be sure his cold fingers would register the difference between metal and snow. He brushed his hands clean and plunged them into his pockets to warm them back up.

"Keep expectations low, and things are a lot less disappointing." Tim seemed to be talking for his own benefit, but Gannon checked the drive, not far off.

The lead singer stopped and flashed his light in their manager's face. "Awestruck never would've succeeded if we'd taken that lousy advice. Why would we lower our expectations when it comes to the people who matter?"

Tim lifted a hand to shield his eyes.

Gannon resumed his search. "We'll find the necklace."

His commitment and certainty instilled hope in Philip, but forty-five minutes later, reality regained its chokehold. If not for the snow, they'd have a chance, but so much of it blanketed the ground. So much. The locket was less than an inch across, and they didn't even know if she'd lost it outside. Everyone was tired and ought to be able to celebrate Christmas instead of wandering around in the cold and the snow on a fool's errand. The necklace, like the woman it represented, was gone. The sooner he came to terms with that, the sooner he could come up with a permanent plan to cope.

He opened his mouth to call off the search, but a surge of emotion forced him to raise his knuckles silently to his lips instead. He tried again. Same result. He was about ten seconds from tears, so he started for the closest shelter.

~

"You want to go, or should I?"

Gannon swung his focus from the fort wall to John, who stood by him, eyes trained on Philip's SUV.

John tipped his head toward the vehicle. "He isn't looking for a necklace in there."

Gannon straightened. As they'd cleaned up after the meal, Adeline had whispered her concern that Philip was sad.

"Will you check on him?" she'd asked.

Philip had seemed all right to Gannon during dinner, but he wasn't about to refuse Adeline, so he'd nodded. He hadn't had the chance to broach the topic with Philip before he put the kids to bed.

Now, Gannon had missed whatever raised John's suspicions,

but the guy usually wasn't wrong about things like this. Philip certainly had looked off when he'd come in the living room and announced he needed help. "What's he upset about? Not a locket."

John shrugged.

"Together?" Gannon asked. They'd have a better shot at lending comfort if they both worked on the right thing to say.

John wordlessly started for the vehicle, and Gannon followed suit. They opened the back doors. Sure enough, Philip sat in the last row. John climbed in and sat next to him. Gannon took a seat in the center row.

No one said anything.

Only John didn't seem to mind the silence, leaning back against the headrest, eyes nearly closed while Gannon prayed for words that might help. None came to him.

"Our family was like a weight we were both carrying. Not a bad weight. Just challenging, I guess, but we loved being a family." Grief strained Philip's voice, but at least he wasn't sobbing. "Now she's gone, and I'm left shouldering the whole load. It's like looking for a necklace that's not going to be found. She's gone, and it's been almost five years, and it still ..."

Being on tour must've given him a reprieve, because this was the first Gannon had realized Philip still hurt this much over losing Clare.

"I can't imagine," John said.

Not eloquent, but it was true for Gannon too. He and Adeline had been estranged for years, but he'd always held out hope that one day they'd reconcile. What would it have been like to not have hope of a reunion this side of eternity?

Tim stuck his head in. "What are you ...?" He frowned and settled into the middle row with Gannon.

Minutes ticked by, and Philip wiped his face with the back of his hand. A few more minutes. Tim shifted.

"I guess we should go in so the others can stop looking," Philip said.

Gannon felt the atmosphere changing, Philip gathering his courage. The time for silently sitting had passed.

"I'd never suggest this will fix everything," Gannon said. "But we're here for you. If we can help shoulder that weight, we're going to."

Philip swallowed hard and stared at the floor. "Thanks." He leaned forward, which felt like a signal, and they all climbed out of the SUV. John rested a hand on Philip's shoulder as they started for the cabin.

∼

IT WAS nine thirty on Christmas Eve, and Adeline was more than ready to be done looking for the necklace, but if the guys were still searching the yard, she couldn't very well give up.

Besides, she hurt for Philip and Nila and wanted to help.

Even if it meant sacrificing time with Gannon.

She shouldn't have to remind herself of that continuously.

She nudged Bruce, who was following her from spot to spot, out of the way and lifted the entryway rug in case the locket had slipped underneath. Some dust speckled the tile, but no necklace.

Bruce, apparently as tired of the search as Adeline, eyed her then ambled off.

As she replaced the mat, she found herself humming "Amazing Grace."

Philip said the song brought Nila comfort, but given what the melody seemed to do to Philip, she'd have to be careful not to let the notes rise in her throat near him.

Still, the song and the idea that it comforted Nila stuck with her as she opened the coat closet and moved the collection of shoes, checking the floor.

Music could do that. Bring healing.

It'd been an integral part of Adeline's own story. What could be more meaningful than sharing that gift with a hurting child?

She sat back on her heels.

Really, what could be?

Instead of searching for a remote job, she could travel with the band and host workshops for local kids.

Or not. She resumed the search.

Ten minutes hadn't offered Nila much healing, hadn't given her the skills to incorporate music into her life beyond their brief time together. Even if the workshops lasted an hour or a half day, without ongoing support, the lessons wouldn't take root.

With a sigh, Adeline picked up the little girl's boots and reached inside in case the necklace had fallen in.

Nope. She plunged her hand into Nason's right boot.

Her fingers touched something cool and textured.

As soon as her eyes confirmed what her hand felt, she dropped the boot and stepped out of the closet. "Got it!"

The front door clattered into the closet door, the guys entering in time to hear her declaration.

Philip seemed shocked into stillness. He looked from Adeline to the locket before holding out his hand. He said nothing, just swallowed hard.

The guys slapped his shoulders.

Grinning, Gannon turned to Tim, who'd tailed them inside. "What did I tell you?"

Whatever that was about, even Tim smiled. "Yeah, go on."

Philip closed his hand around the locket. "I'll go put this somewhere safe. Be right back."

Everyone settled back into the living room for their makeshift Christmas Eve service. When Philip returned, they took turns reading through the Christmas account in Luke, and Gannon led them in a few Christmas songs.

In about thirty-six hours, he'd be gone again. She'd be on her own without a plan for a better future.

But for now, his voice rose from right next to her, a powerful reminder of the real reason for Christmas: Jesus, come to find the lost.

12

*a*t six, Philip opened his eyes to find Nila and Nason at his bedside, peering at him.

Clare is gone, and the kids are here.

But the loss didn't hit as hard as the night before, not with the kids standing close, hope welling in their eyes. Their hope wasn't for his attention. They wanted presents. Nonetheless, they aimed their hope at him because he was the one who'd provide for them now.

He had a pile of presents waiting for them, and beyond today, he would find a way to meet their other needs too. He would come up with the plan his dad advised him to make.

"Can we go now?" Nason asked.

Nila tugged the hand he'd rested on the covers. "Grandpa said when you wake up, you'll take us to our presents."

They would open their gifts at the new house, an hour and a half from here. He focused on the clock again. Beside it on the bedside table lay the locket.

He stretched to reach it and motioned his daughter closer. "Look what we found."

As her gaze found the necklace, she sucked a breath through her teeth and danced with glee.

She watched him open the clasp, then pivoted and pressed the pendant to her chest as he fastened the chain. Finished, he brushed her hair out from under the sterling silver.

"Beautiful," he said.

She opened the heart-shaped locket and looked inside. "Like Mom?"

"Just like your mother."

Nason edged in. "Do I get something too?"

"You both get piles of presents." He mussed his son's hair, though it looked like he'd already met with a brush this morning. "Go wait with Grandma and Grandpa. I'll be ready in a minute."

Aware they'd get less and less patient, he hurried to join them, and they left the cabin before six thirty without seeing any of the others. By eight, he'd parked in the driveway of a house that could star in a Christmas painting, thanks to the sunshine, the blanket of snow, and the evergreen wreath on the door. He unlocked the door and pointed the kids toward the living room.

They ran ahead while Philip and his parents glanced into the rooms along the way. Movers had relocated his belongings and unpacked. An interior designer had also been at work, choosing furnishings to fill out the space. The result was trendy and modern without tipping over the line where the kids would have to worry about breaking things every time they turned around.

After Christmas, Dad and Joan would pack up the kids' belongings and move them here. When the tour ended, all Philip would have to do was come home to them. And figure out how to do life with a pair of kids he didn't really know who needed care he couldn't provide.

But he'd learn. Clare was gone, and he needed to step up.

They entered the broad, light-soaked living room. A tree, fully decked out, stood before tall windows that looked out over the snowy yard. Philip plugged in the lights and hurried to snap a picture of the kids staring at the piles of wrapped gifts—the moment of awe wouldn't last long.

"It's beautiful," Joan breathed.

Nila turned toward him, a gift in her hands, a plea on her face. Nason crouched to claim a present for himself. Philip took another picture, gave Nila the go-ahead to open the box she held, and helped Nason locate one of his.

A sense of control he hadn't felt since being reunited with the kids grew each time their faces lit up at their gifts. He'd consulted Dad and Joan, but Philip had been the one to approve what his assistant bought and wrapped. The result was sheer delight on the kids' faces.

This was the solution, as evidenced by the fully furnished home around them and the joy in Nason's and Nila's squeals. Thanks to Awestruck, he could hire out what he couldn't do himself.

Nila bumped into his knee, a small box in her hand. "This is for you, Daddy."

"You got me something?"

"Oh!" Nason popped up from the robot he'd just unwrapped and scampered to Joan.

She presented him with a thin gift-wrapped item about the size of a sheet of paper, which the boy carried to Philip. Nason stood ramrod straight, waiting with the packet in his hands as Philip loosened the paper on the box Nila had given him. Inside a jewelry box, on a bed of cotton, lay a polymer clay guitar.

"Just like yours," Nila said.

"Thank you. You made this for me?"

She nodded, and he pulled her into a hug. It actually looked like a bass guitar. She was growing up. In no time, she'd be an adult. He just needed to do his job and set her loose. He kissed the top of her head and released her to the last of her own presents, then accepted Nason's offering.

Since it felt like the gift was paper, he removed the wrapping carefully. Sure enough, the wrapping covered a manila folder. He hefted Nason onto his lap. His son had drawn a gray house—the same color as the house they sat in now—and three stick figures with big, smiling faces.

"That's you." Nason pointed to the biggest of the three, the one wearing what Philip guessed was a guitar. Next, he tapped his finger on the pink figure, and the one hanging like a monkey from the branches of a tree. "Nila, and me."

The curved lines representing each of their smiles reached from eye to eye.

"We look very happy," Philip said. "Do you think we're going to be, just the three of us?"

Nason giggled and nodded.

Philip hugged him to his chest and kissed his head as he had Nila's. "I think we'll be happy too."

~

GANNON HAD NEVER MADE SUCH a pretty coffee. He held a mug of plain earl grey tea in his left hand and a mug of chocolate mocha with a swirl of whipped cream and a dusting of red sugar crystals in his right. A drink fit for his girlfriend on Christmas Day.

When he'd woken that morning, she'd already seen Tegan off, headed back to Lakeshore to spend Christmas with her fiancé. Soon, Gannon and Adeline would leave for their hometown. John would ride with them, since all of their families lived there and he no longer had Nicole to share the drive with.

Tomorrow morning, Awestruck would reconvene, and he'd leave Adeline to finish out the tour. She'd spend a week with her parents, and they'd drive her home again while Gannon rang in the new year with thousands of strangers.

Fans. Fans he was grateful for.

But even with the end of the tour in sight, just a couple of weeks into January, he'd never wanted to cancel shows as much as he did right now.

Instead, he'd make the most of the time he had. Tim was sleeping, and John had ventured out with the dogs, while Adeline waited for Gannon on the couch closest to the decorated tree. Thousands of tiny white lights lit the branches, but their glow couldn't compete with the golden morning sun slanting through the room.

Adeline, in her cozy sweater with a plaid blanket drawn across her lap, and Bruce lounging nearby, looked perfect here, and regret that this wasn't their life—not permanently, anyway —pulled him toward her, to be as close as possible for as long as possible.

She accepted the coffee and a kiss that didn't last nearly long enough. He sat beside her as she slid the mug onto the table without sipping his creation. She grasped a small gift box and fidgeted. Nervous?

"You know whatever it is, I'll love it."

Her fleeting smile said she wasn't so sure. "You bought me three basses and whatever you saved for this morning. This does not compete."

"It's not a competition." He slipped a lock of her hair behind her ear and couldn't resist letting his fingers run through the silky strands as he pulled his hand away. "I would never see you or anything you gave me as less-than."

"I know." She smoothed her hand over the black-and-gold gift wrap. "It's only that we haven't had a lot of chances this year to show each other ... It seems like I haven't had enough chances to show you what you mean to me, and some chances I had, I let little things make me angry instead of enjoying our time together."

Oh no. Were those tears? He took her hand.

Her glance was fleeting. "It's just really hard to say goodbye all the time."

The separations killed him too. He touched her jaw and pressed a gentle kiss to her lips.

"Maybe this will help." He rose to take his gift for her from under the tree, and a pang in his gut evened the playing field. Maybe he was nervous too.

As soon as he sat back down, Adeline handed him the gift she'd held. He followed suit, but she inclined her head, eyes on the present she'd given him.

So much for ladies first. He ran his finger under the seam of the gift wrap. Inside was a box, and inside that, a leather-bound notebook the size of a novel.

"This way, you can stop writing lyrics in the same spiral notebooks you used in high school."

"So you noticed the math notes in the one I let you keep."

Her smile lit her eyes the way the sun lit the room.

He'd given her that notebook, one dedicated to lyrics he'd written about her, about a year and a half ago. Since then, he'd taken to writing on whatever scraps were available. He'd typed some lyrics on his phone too, but it was long past time for a new designated place for his work. He ran his hand over the cover and flipped through the pages.

Inside the flap, she'd written: *To Gannon from Adeline with love.*

She'd ended the simple inscription with the date.

She leaned closer, as if to reread it. "You're the writer, not me."

"It's perfect." He savored another kiss before settling the book on his lap and motioning for her to open the gift he'd picked up in Chicago. Those poor little tree seeds had a lot riding on them, given he hoped they'd help comfort her in the face of their next parting, now one day away.

She freed the gift from the decorative bag and pulled away the tissue paper. Her eyebrows came down with focus, and then a smile lit her features. "A spruce tree growing kit?"

He took one of her hands. "You didn't always get my best this year. And I didn't get to see you nearly as much as I would've liked, but the tour ends in January, and next year will be better. We'll see each other almost every day, and by the time the next tour comes around, I really hope you'll be my wife."

She quietly nodded and squeezed his hand, and relief lifted some of his worry.

At least she wasn't hedging because of their rough patch— or veering the opposite direction and asking why he wasn't proposing right now.

Marriage could only serve as part of the solution. The other part demanded they find a way to handle his travel that worked for both of them. If he had his way, he would've taken her along this year, set up a seat for her in the wings of all his shows, made sure she always had the room next to his.

Which might've led to poor choices.

But next time ...

"If we're married," he said, "we won't have to say good night, let alone goodbye."

Her cheeks flushed at the implications. She lifted the gift. "What does all this have to do with spruce trees?"

"In April, when you showed me that tree you planted in your front yard, you said you were putting down roots. Remember that?"

"I regretted it as soon as I said it. I was afraid putting down roots here would mean you and I would be apart."

"But I'm moving here, so it doesn't. From now on, I'd like us to find a way to put down roots together. You can start this tree in its pot. Then, when you and I do get married, we can plant it by our front door."

Adeline turned the pot so the growing directions faced her. "I like that plan." She glanced at him, then studied the packaging a little longer.

"What?"

"I checked online for remote job openings so I could travel more but didn't see anything." She ran her finger along a ridge of the tin the spruce seeds came in. "Then yesterday, right before dinner, Nila told me her mom used to love 'Amazing Grace,' so we played it together. Philip heard and said something about how much comfort she'd found in the song, and it got me thinking about how much music has meant to me." Finally, she peeled her gaze away from the gift. A passion he hadn't seen in months lit her eyes. "To us."

He nodded and resisted pulling her in for another kiss so he could hear the idea that had her this excited.

"Everybody who wants should have a chance at that. Hurting kids, especially."

Patience expiring as he caught her meaning, he wrapped an arm around her and settled her against him. "You want to do something about it."

"Not all families can afford music lessons. Even taking band or orchestra through a school can be expensive. But if I'm traveling with you more, I wouldn't be here to teach all the time. So I was thinking I could spend this year getting a non-profit up and running to provide music lessons to kids who might not get them otherwise. Even when we're traveling, I'd have a role with it—something so I would have meaningful work—but I'd hire someone else to run the day-to-day so details wouldn't tie me down away from you."

He kissed the top of her head. "I know someone who'd fund a place like that."

"You think I should go for it? I can fundraise. The bill doesn't have to fall to you."

Gannon laughed. "If this is how we get to spend more time together, that'll be the best funded music studio around."

She tilted her head and glanced up at him. "You say that like you missed me."

He tucked her hair behind her ear, leaning closer to the smile playing on her lips. "You say that like you're surprised." He kissed the corner of her mouth. "Haven't I convinced you I love you yet?"

Amusement flickered, rounding her cheeks. The warmth in her eyes contradicted the shake of her head. She knew he loved her, and she was so secure in that, she'd tease him.

He'd have it no other way.

He rested his forehead against hers. "I drove all night through a blizzard to get here. I had three upright basses delivered and waiting. I gave a great speech about putting down roots. What more will it take?"

She brushed the tip of her nose against his. "How about a kiss?"

He obliged as if he could prove his love that way, but as much as having her in his arms meant to him, as much as he lost himself in the feel of her lips on his, a kiss would never prove his dedication to her, just like no gift he could've gotten her would have.

But that was okay. He didn't need to put all of his dedication in a gift or a kiss when he had the rest of his life to prove how serious he was about loving her well.

～

JOHN REARRANGED the luggage and gifts in the back of the SUV. Since he, Gannon, Adeline, and all three dogs would all be riding home to Fox Valley together, they needed most of the seats clear. Once all the baggage fit, he went in for the dogs.

"All set?" Adeline pressed the lid on a travel mug and extended it to him.

Tim sat at the dining table, reading on a tablet and sipping coffee. "See you guys tomorrow."

"You sure you don't want to come with?" Gannon shrugged into his coat.

"Positive. I'm looking forward to a day all to myself." Tim took another draw from his coffee cup. "I've had enough of you guys."

If he'd spoken with any more cheer in his voice, Adeline probably would've gotten offended on their behalf, but John understood where it was coming from. Touring meant a lot of time in close quarters. If not for the major holiday, John wouldn't mind finding a few blissful hours of silence alone in a cabin in the middle of nowhere for himself.

Today, Tim was the lucky one.

John led his dogs outside and started hooking them into safety harnesses that would keep them in the back row. Meanwhile, Adeline settled Bruce where he could lay on the floor in the middle, then she and Gannon took places in front.

"So, this coat was a gift to her?"

John glanced over his shoulder to see Adeline twisted in her seat, the jacket he'd given Nicole in her hands. Gannon must've told her, because the question sounded rhetorical.

John would rather not make a bigger deal of the breakup than it already was, but the more closely she looked at the coat, the bigger of a deal it would be. Maybe if he acted as if she wasn't close to a discovery, she'd lose interest.

He refocused on clasping the harness across Camo's chest. When he finished with the dogs and settled into his own seat behind Adeline, she still held the coat, and now Gannon watched him in the rearview mirror. Even Bruce, lounging on the floor next to him, seemed concerned for him.

John leaned and saw the glitter of diamonds in Adeline's hands.

So they'd found the earrings Nicole hadn't taken the time to discover. He slid the coat from Adeline's grasp and held out his other hand.

She lay the earrings in his palm, curious brown eyes fixed on him. "Are you okay?"

"Mostly, I'm glad she didn't bother to try it on." If she had, she would've put her hands in the pockets and found the earrings. She would've recognized the jewelry as nicer than the bracelet and she might not've come clean.

Peering back at him, Adeline rested her cheek against the side of her seat. "I'm sorry it turned out this way."

"Me too."

But Nicole hadn't been the one for him.

Compared with Philip's grief over losing his wife—still raw after five years—what he and Nicole had wasn't even a blip on the radar. John would hold out for the real thing.

Now if only Adeline would stop gazing at him with such pity.

He zipped the earrings back in the pocket and laid the coat on the seat next to him. "Like Gannon said, we shouldn't lower our expectations when it comes to the people who matter."

She raised an eyebrow at her boyfriend. "You said that?"

Gannon started the SUV with a shrug and a grin. "I say all kinds of insightful things."

John settled in his seat and watched the cabin disappear behind the trees. Raising his expectations might mean holding out for someone who didn't know about his money, at least not at first. He might have trouble finding that kind of anonymity in LA or while on tour, but in a rural section of a relatively quiet state?

It could happen.

The house he'd toured yesterday fit the plan.

He sent his real estate agent a text, asking her to put in an offer.

The quiet setting would be a refuge. That alone would justify the purchase, but the house also fit who he wanted to be and what he valued. He didn't want notoriety and an impressive exterior as much as he wanted truth and authenticity. He wanted something that stood the test of time.

Given the complications—his money, the inevitable scars his experience with Nicole would leave—he might have more trouble finding those things in a relationship than he'd encountered finding a house, but he'd hold out for her.

Doubt snaked in. Did she exist?

Adeline turned the radio to Christmas tunes, reminding John what day it was.

Things hadn't gone his way with Nicole, but what he'd thought even before leaving Chicago remained true.

If ever there was a time for hope, this was it.

~

For to us a child is born,
to us a son is given;
and the government shall be upon his shoulder,
and his name shall be called
Wonderful Counselor, Mighty God,
Everlasting Father, Prince of Peace.
Isaiah 9:6, ESV

Spend more time in Lakeshore with an email subscriber exclusive.

Food trailer owner Asher has seen too many tears he couldn't dry. Determined to be part of the solution, he avoids romance and all the heartbreaking drama that comes along with it.

At least, that's the plan until his heart decides it has a mind of its own. If he can't rein it in, he's destined to break not one but two women's hearts.

Subscribers to Emily's email newsletters will have the opportunity to download *Between the Two of Us*, which is a prequel novella to the Rhythms of Redemption Romances, as a welcome gift.

Subscribers will also be the first to receive updates about new releases in the Rhythms of Redemption Romance series.

Sign up at emilyconradauthor.com.

DISCUSSION GUIDE

1. Have you ever gone to great lengths to spend time with a loved one? Share about your experience.
2. What celebrity might you approach for an autograph or picture, if you recognized him or her in public?
3. What gifts were given during the story? Which do you think was most valuable to the recipient?
4. Gannon gave Adeline a personal gift that Nicole felt was strange. Have you ever given or received a sentimental gift that might have seemed odd to others?
5. Whose storyline were you most invested in? Why?
6. Have you ever been in a long-distance relationship? What advice would you give Gannon and Adeline?
7. Philip is daunted by the responsibility of caring for his kids. Have you ever felt like God gave you more than you could handle? What helped you in those circumstances?
8. Do you agree that John not wanting to open up

about his past is different than Nicole not telling
him about her debt? Why or why not?

9. Philip, John, and Matt each found a resolution of
   sorts by the end of the novella, but they also each
   have some obstacles left to overcome. What
   potential conflicts can you identify that might play
   into their stories? Whose story are you most looking
   forward to?

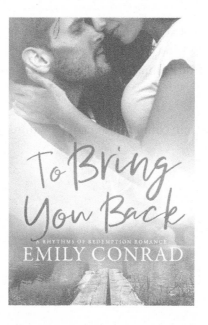

Find out how it all began in *To Bring You Back*

He's determined to confront the past she's desperate to forget.

When Adeline Green's now-famous high school crush descends on her quiet life, a public spotlight threatens to expose her deepest regret. After eight years of trying to bury her mistakes under a life of service, she's broke financially and spiritually. The last thing she can afford is feelings for the man who took center stage in her past—even if he does claim to know the secret to her redemption.

Gannon Vaughn and his rock band, Awestruck, have conquered the music industry, but he can't overcome his feelings for Adeline. When he hears she's struggling, he sets out to turn her life around and win back the love he lost to poor choices eight years ago.

But when Gannon's fame and their mutual regrets jeopar-

Find out how it all began!

dize their relationship anew, will grace be enough to bring them back to God and each other?

Available from Amazon, Barnes and Noble, and other retailers.

Learn more at emilyconradauthor.com/rhythmsofredemption/

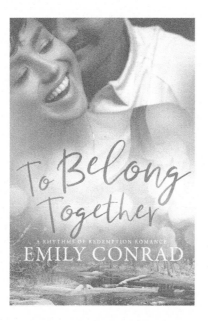

To Belong Together - Book 2 - Drummer John Kennedy can keep
a beat, but he can't hold a conversation, so he relies on actions
to show he cares. Unfortunately, when he's instantly intrigued
by a spunky female mechanic, he can't seem to convey to
sincerity of his intentions.

Erin Hirsh is convinced a rock star with a supermodel ex can't
possibly see anything in her - until they find common ground
in faith and their worsening family situations. Could God
intend this pair of opposites to belong together?

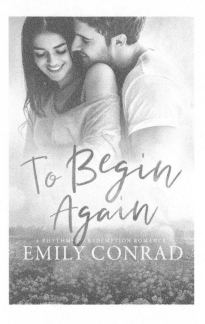

To Begin Again - Book 3 - Whatever faith Philip Miller had died with his wife. Now, "Amazing Grace" is nothing but a lullaby to sing to his children in her memory. With a dark secret already threatening his family's future, he has no intention of finding love again. If only he weren't so drawn to pop star Michaela Vandehey, who is in Lakeshore to collaborate with Awestruck.

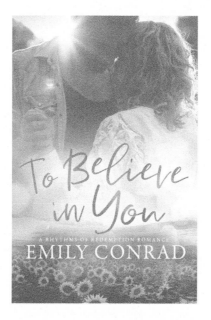

To Believe In You - Book 4 - Since his dismissal from the rock band Awestruck, former bassist and addict Matt Visser has been transformed by faith and a year of sobriety. If he can repay his parents for one last major debt, he can move into the future with a clear conscience. But just as he wins the trust of his beautiful but cautious coworker, Lina Abbey, a new truth about Matt's past reveals a wrong he can never right. Both he and Lina both need something more trustworthy than Matt to believe in. Otherwise, history will repeat itself in all the worst ways.

Subscribe to emails for updates on new releases and find all the latest on the series at https://www. EmilyConradAuthor.com/RhythmsofRedemption.

ACKNOWLEDGMENTS

In the editing of this novella, I discovered that Wisconsin has given me some experiences that aren't universal. So, I'd like to thank my Midwestern upbringing for puppy chow, snowstorms, and rural drives.

My husband named Jacked and Twisted. Hooray, Adam! Thank you for informing so much of what I write in so many ways.

To my editors, critique partners, beta readers, and proofreaders, thank you! Special thanks to Robin Patchen, Judy DeVries, Robyn Hook, Jessica Bradley, Sarah Strong, Kendra Arthur, and Jane Bradley. It's because of you that the story has extra Christmas cheer, gift wrap didn't magically change colors, poor Bruce didn't up and disappear, and so much more.

Awestruck's fan club used to be just one member strong. Fandom is absolutely better with friends. Thanks for reading these stories and caring about these characters.

Jesus, no one has ever gone to greater lengths than you to spend time with me. Thank you for righting what went wrong in our relationship when I could not and for ensuring I could spend not only Christmas with you, but all of eternity.

ABOUT THE AUTHOR

Emily Conrad writes contemporary Christian romance that explores life's relevant questions. Though she likes to think some of her characters are pretty great, the ultimate hero of her stories (including the one she's living) is Jesus. She lives in Wisconsin with her husband and their energetic coonhound rescue. Learn more about her and her books at emily-conradauthor.com.

facebook.com/emilyconradauthor

twitter.com/emilyrconrad

instagram.com/emilyrconrad

ALSO BY EMILY CONRAD

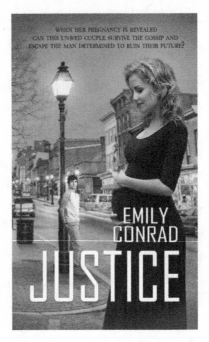

The love of a lifetime, a quest for justice, and redemption that can only be found by faith.

DID YOU ENJOY THIS BOOK?

Help others discover it by leaving a review on Goodreads and the site you purchased from!

Made in the USA
Las Vegas, NV
15 May 2022

48926520R00083